McKEAG'S
MOUNTAIN

Also by L. J. Martin
in Large Print:

The Benicia Belle
The Devil's Bounty
Shadow of the Grizzly
Stranahan
Wolf Mountain

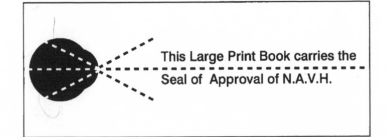

McKEAG'S MOUNTAIN

L. J. MARTIN

Thorndike Press • Waterville, Maine

Published in 2005 by arrangement with Pinnacle Books, an imprint of Kensington Publishing Corp.

Thorndike Press® Large Print Western.

The tree indicium is a trademark of Thorndike Press.

The text of this Large Print edition is unabridged.
Other aspects of the book may vary from the original edition.

Set in 16 pt. Plantin by Ramona Watson.

Printed in the United States on permanent paper.

Library of Congress Cataloging-in-Publication Data

Martin, Larry Jay.
    McKeag's Mountain / by L.J. Martin.
        p. cm. — (Thorndike Press large print western)
    Originally published: New York : Kensington Pub., c2004, in series: Pinnacle western.
    ISBN 0-7862-8068-9 (lg. print : hc : alk. paper)
    1. Ranchers — Fiction.   2. Revenge — Fiction.
3. Montana — Fiction.   4. Large type books.   I. Title.
II. Thorndike Press large print Western series.
PS3563.A72487M37 2005
    813′.54—dc22   2005020007

To Edward P. Fischer, M.D.
Like me, 150 years too late.
An uncommon man.

As the Founder/CEO of NAVH, the only national health agency solely devoted to those who, although not totally blind, have an eye disease which could lead to serious visual impairment, I am pleased to recognize Thorndike Press* as one of the leading publishers in the large print field.

Founded in 1954 in San Francisco to prepare large print textbooks for partially seeing children, NAVH became the pioneer and standard setting agency in the preparation of large type.

Today, those publishers who meet our standards carry the prestigious "Seal of Approval" indicating high quality large print. We are delighted that Thorndike Press is one of the publishers whose titles meet these standards. We are also pleased to recognize the significant contribution Thorndike Press is making in this important and growing field.

Lorraine H. Marchi, L.H.D.
Founder/CEO
NAVH

* Thorndike Press encompasses the following imprints: Thorndike, Wheeler, Walker and Large Print Press.

Chapter 1

Helena, Montana, 1877

"Silas, this is a rare opportunity. The drought in eastern Washington and Oregon means every cow's for sale . . . cheap . . . and I've got grass going to waste. I need that five thousand. . . ." Dan McKeag reclined in the ladder-back chair and eyed his old friend and banker with deep blue eyes that could turn to slate ice at times. Across the desk, Dan sat quiet, still as a cougar waiting to pounce, wanting an answer from the president of the Helena Stockmen and Merchants Bank.

The banker scratched muttonchop side-whiskers, then folded his hands in his lap. "Dan, I can't do it. The board —"

McKeag's voice dropped an octave. "The board take the hindmost, Silas. This is between you and me. It's always been between you and me."

Silas also sat back, saying nothing in reply. Suddenly the wide oak desk seemed a chasm as large as the Missouri, which flowed only a few miles from where they eyed each other in Helena, Montana.

Dan McKeag sighed, running his hand through his thick black hair, knowing he wasn't going to get the money and why, so he rose and secured his broad-brimmed hat squarely on his head, his blue eyes going to ice. "So, that's it? That's the sum total of over ten years of my paying my debts to this bank on time, most times early?"

Silas Bingham rose also, and extended his hand across the desk. "Dan, you get through this . . . this current problem, then you come back and see me."

"So Old Man Prager's got his claws in you too?" McKeag asked accusingly.

But Silas didn't answer, and his silence was answer enough.

For old time's sake, Dan went ahead and took the banker's slim hand and shook. But he wasn't about to let the subject lie, so he pressed. "Exactly what problem would I have, Silas?"

"You know what problem."

"You say it. You're turning me down . . . so you say it."

The banker cut his eyes away, then collapsed and leaned way back in his chair.

"Dan, there are a half-dozen rough-cut men in Helena —"

"Seven, I've heard."

"Seven then. Men unknown to us townfolk. Outsiders. Rumor is . . . they're here to kill you."

Dan McKeag chuckled. "They don't have that kind of bark on them, Silas. You know damned well, it's been tried by many. Many rougher than any the Bar X can hire." Dan McKeag hunkered forward, leaning both ham-sized scarred fists on the oak desk, and his voice became low and gravelly. "Many rough-and-tumble old boys have tried to shoot me down, and before that my old man, and before him, old Sean McKeag. McKeags seem to take a lot of killing. That's only one of the reasons we've always been a good credit risk."

Silas seemed to redden a little, then cleared his throat before he responded. "I'd suggest you find a quiet way out, Dan. The back way, if you would. We don't want that kind of trouble here at the bank."

McKeag said sardonically, his blue eyes unreadable, "Well, Silas old friend, why don't you just reach in that bottom drawer of yours and strap on that hogleg you keep there. Then you and me'll walk over to Cutter's Saloon or the Montana Club, and

I'll buy you a drink . . . just to show you there's no hard feelings."

Again, the banker reddened, then picked up some papers and began to shuffle them into a square stack. "I've got enough hard work here to last me a —"

"Turning down old friends *is* hard work, I imagine. Hope you sleep well, Silas." With that, McKeag turned and started for the door. But he stopped short, someone blocking his way.

The man in front of him, a head shorter than the cattleman but just as broad in the shoulders, was well known to Dan McKeag, was in fact related if marriage counted. But they hadn't spoken in eight years. Dan had walked right by him at the bank's door on the way in, as they'd passed many times before in years past . . . hadn't spoken since the day Dan had taken Erin Dundee, the man's sister, in matrimony against the wishes of her brother, Padraig. The shorter man wore a brass badge and carried a sawed-off double-barreled shotgun casually in the crook of his thick arm. He wore a revolver low on his right side, butt forward.

"Dan," Padraig Dundee said, as if they had just had a pleasant dinner the night before, as if the eight strained years had never happened.

McKeag pulled up short, and eyed the shorter man for a long moment before he spoke. "Pad . . . you decide to bury the hatchet?"

"If it was up to me, Dan old boy, I'd bury one in yer ugly noggin, but I'd never have a peaceful moment if'n I did." Paddy laughed — the crooked smile hadn't changed — then turned serious. "Thought you might need some company today. Looks like it might storm outside."

"It's clear as a mountain stream out there, Pad. I can handle the weather."

Pad Dundee snickered again, and he reached up with his free hand and tugged on a cauliflowered earlobe. "It would pain me little sister, Danny me boy, should you get swept away by a stiff wind, or high water, or a load of buckshot, so I believe I'll just limp along."

The banker rose again, glowering. "You're on duty, Dundee. You've got business right here."

Pad Dundee had been a bank guard at the Helena Stockman and Merchants for over a year, the only job he could find after taking a .45-70 to the leg while riding shotgun for the express company, but he dismissed the banker with a wave of his hand as if it was nothing. "Then I believe I

11

quit, Mr. Bingham. I'll be walking my brother-in-law over to have a mug."

For the third time that afternoon, the banker's face reddened. "There won't be any coming back, Dundee. You leave your duty —"

Paddy Dundee counted on his fingers as Bingham spoke, then interrupted. "I'll be having the eight dollars you owe me, if that's the case. I was thinkin' about quittin' yesterday . . . when I saw you kowtowin' to Old Man Prager."

Silas Bingham puffed up like a tabby cat facing a coyote, but said nothing, only spun on his heel.

Dundee and McKeag stood in silence as the banker stalked over into a teller's cage, drew the money out, returned, then handed it to the bank guard, who removed his badge and stuffed the brass implement into the banker's waistcoat watch pocket.

Then Pad Dundee tipped his hat to Bingham. "It's been a pleasure guardin' your money, Mr. Bingham." Then he turned to Dan McKeag. "This'll be enough to buy us a thick steak and all the trimmin's, and a good deal to spare . . . should we live till supper time."

"You don't need to do this, Pad."

"Yes, Dan, I do. I've been studyin' on this since yesterday, and I'm comin' along, you like it or not. Let's go see what the dogs dragged in."

Chapter 2

Dan McKeag reached for the bank's leaded glass door, but Paddy Dundee stopped him short.

"Let me wander out first, Dan." Without waiting for Dan to answer, Pad stepped in front of him and slipped into the doorway without fully opening it. He was only halfway out when he glanced back. "What a coincidence. Seems Old Man Prager has picked the bank's own bench to have his ornery old self a smoke."

Paddy moved on out and down to the corner of the building, away from where the old man sat, and carefully eyed the board-walks and the roof-lines across the brick street.

No wonder Bingham wanted me to go out the back way. He knew Old Man Prager was waiting. McKeag hoisted his Remington just a little to make sure it rode free and easy in its holster, then stepped out and turned toward the old man, who rose and glowered, leaning on his cane, a corncob pipe stuffed in his mouth over a tobacco-stained salt-and-pepper beard. He was the only man Dan had known to smoke and chew at the same time.

Dan's cow dog, Blue, ninety-five pounds of half-Irish wolfhound and, Dan suspected, half-timber wolf, rose from where he'd been lying waiting for his master's return, and paced Dan. He lowered his head as if on the prowl, and the hair on the back of his thick neck bristled. The low rumble of a growl made the old man cut his eyes down at the big mutt.

McKeag had no thought that Prager would draw on him, even though the old man wore a small, brand-new Smith and Wesson .41-caliber Thunderer strapped on his hip. It was Prager's rumored seven hirelings Dan was worried about. But it was obvious that Prager wanted a word with him. That was just fine with Dan, as he had some words for the old man.

"Didn't get no money, did you, neighbor?" Prager asked, his tone friendly enough, but his rummy eyes, deep-set in a well-lined, pockmarked face seemingly carved from weathered granite, glistened with hate.

"Seems you had something to do with that," Dan said, walking up so he stood al-

15

most chest-to-chest with the old man. At one time, Prager had been an imposing man, tall as Dan's six feet, and broad through the chest and shoulders, but now he was stinted and beginning to wither. He'd failed badly over the last year, after Dan McKeag had blown his low-life son into the dry dust bed of Spotted Dog Creek.

Prager was growing old, but he still had the snarl of a cougar. "That's only the beginning of yer woes, Dan McKeag, if'n yer not ready to sell out to me."

Blue continued the low rumble.

Prager snapped, "Shut that mangy mutt up, before I send him to hound-dog hell."

Dan ignored his comment about the dog; in fact, he growled almost as low as the hound. "You haven't enough money to buy me out, Bertoldus, even if I was inclined."

No one other than Dan McKeag ever called Bertoldus Prager by his full given name. All called him Bert, which he preferred; in fact, he'd been known to fight when called Bertoldus. Dan knew it was one of many things that perturbed the old man, and enjoyed the fact. Blue continued his low rumble.

Prager's eyes sparked as he cut them

back to Dan. "Is seven yer lucky number, McKeag?"

"My old granddaddy wouldn't have named the McKeag place the Lucky Seven if it weren't, Bertoldus."

"And winnin' that land in a poker game was the only way a worthless McKeag would have gotten it. Well, seven won't be lucky for the McKeags afore this day is out . . . fact is, it'll be *my* lucky number from now on."

Dan gave him a lazy smile. "You should know, Bertoldus, cane or no cane, that when I finish with the scum I hear are smellin' up Helena, I'll be comin' to the Bar X to pay you a visit . . . and it won't be a social one."

Prager turned his head enough that when he spit the tobacco he chewed, it missed McKeag's boot by only a few inches and fell at Blue's feet. The hound's growl deepened and he bared his teeth, but the old man ignored him. Dan felt his blood run hot, but he said nothing.

"I don't think I'll be losin' any sleep worrying about that, McKeag. You should know, if'n I *was* to hire some men to clean the varmints out of the Deer Lodge country, they wouldn't be no wet-behind-the-ears boys . . . like my son was."

Dan leaned forward, so he was within inches of the corncob pipe Prager had shoved back into his mouth. "Prager, your boy was a back-shootin' coward, well over his majority, who couldn't hit my broad back at twenty paces. And you diverting the Spotted Dog, his lousy upbringing, and his poor shootin' is what got him killed." Dan challenged him again, trying to get the man to admit to his transgressions. "And the way I hear it, you've done hired a handful of worthless scum to do what the Pragers couldn't."

Prager clamped down on the corncob stem hard enough to bite it in half. His jaw muscles knotted under the graying beard, and his eyes seemed to bug out like an angry bull's. Dan half-expected him to paw the ground.

Finally, after a long moment of the two sworn enemies staring at each other, Prager spoke. "Five dollars an acre, McKeag, that's my final offer, and a damn sight more'n that scrub is worth."

"Good! Then there's no more reason to stand here jawing with a foul-smellin' old man."

Dan spun on his heel and walked back past the front door to where Paddy waited. Blue backed away, the hair on his back up, continuing to face the old man until a half-dozen paces back. Paddy had the shotgun hanging casually in his left hand and a big Colt revolver — an old, but well-cared-for, Dragoon .44-caliber converted to percussion — palmed in his right.

Paddy had overheard Prager's offer, and he eyed the old man as he spoke to Dan, not being quite so convinced as McKeag that the old man wouldn't draw the small Thunderer revolver he carried. "So," he said in a low voice, his eyes still on Old Man Prager, "that was a pretty good offer from an old man known to be so tight he'd skin a flea for its hide and tallow. You decide you can't use sixty thousand in good old greenbacks?"

"I wouldn't sell to Prager for ten times that. The Lucky Seven is three generations McKeags. My granddaddy settled that mountain long before there was a Helena or Deer Lodge, and it's gonna be McKeag's Mountain and the Lucky Seven for many generations more. Roan is next in line. Besides, the old bastard's spent his life looking for a puppy dog to kick. As a young'un he was a Michelangelo with a running iron. He's stole most of what he has."

"He ain't no candidate for wings, that's a

sure thing." Pad chewed on what Dan had said for a while, then asked, "You'd leave the Seven to a nephew? Better a son! But not unless you get me sis in a childlike way, Dan." Paddy's tone was condemning, but he grinned, then added, "So, let's head to the Bonny Glen for a mug of that horse piss they call beer."

"Why that doggery, Pad? I'm ready for a glass of good whiskey."

"Most of what they serve would strip the bristles off a swamp-grown boar hog . . . but they got some good too. But the real reason is 'cause that's the part of town where we'll be meeting the problem head on. Scum who take a job like back-shootin' won't be at Mass, or smokin' cigars and hobnobbin' 'bout the price of cattle in the Palace lobby." Paddy gave him that crooked smile, then began to limp around the corner to the wide dirt street leading up the gulch to the saloon, but his eyes continued to sweep the rooftops and entrances off the bricked Reeder's Alley, the narrow climbing passageway where Helena's Bonny Glen was sandwiched between McGoogan's Hotel and Miner's Supply and General Merchandise.

"You think they'll try anything in broad daylight?" McKeag asked as they moved along, keeping close to the storefronts. This was Paddy Dundee's town, and Dan only came this far into civilization when he deemed it absolutely necessary. The Lucky Seven was almost fifty miles west, two hard, grinding days' ride up over the Mullen Pass and down the Little Blackfoot. The ride gave Dan time to think, and to see what other ranches were up to. The little town of Deer Lodge City, only a few miles from the Lucky Seven, had no bank that could handle the loan Dan needed.

"Most of them kind is all gurgle and no guts. I doubt they'll try anything," Paddy said. "Them kind like to slink about in the dark." His eyes still sweeping the street, he continued. "But who knows, Danny boy? Who knows?"

They made the bat-wing doors of the saloon without incident, and after Dan pointed at a spot beside the door and told Blue to lie down, shoved through.

Dan was pleased and surprised to see it a reasonably respectable place, with a sad-eyed old swamper sweeping the already clean floor, the spittoons highly polished, and clean white towels hanging at four-foot spacing under the bar so the patrons could mop beer foam from their mustaches and beards. Cigar and pipe smoke lingered just above head height, and a few goober peanut shells littered the floor in front of where the swamper worked.

There were a dozen men in the place, most miners and drovers by the dress of them, some at the bar, some at tables. Carefully eyeing the men, who had quieted on the two men's arrival, Pad and Dan moved to a table in the far corner, where they could keep backs to the wall and face anything that might come.

Paddy made it clear that he was ready to do business, letting the scattergun clatter to the tabletop, its muzzle ominously facing the crowd.

The crowd returned to talking as a barmaid sauntered across the plank floor. She was dressed like a dance hall girl — even though the place had no music — in red and black, with ample bulges of breasts showing and a skirt at what was considered a disgraceful length just below the knee. Plenty of black-knit stocking showed between high-button shoe and hem. Her hair was piled high, black as a raven's wing, and woven with red ribbons. Her lips had been colored to match the red of the dress.

"What's your pleasure, gents?"

"Knowing your name, missy, would be my pleasure," Paddy said, drawing a smile from Dan and a wink from the woman.

"It would be Shelaugh, whether it pleasures you or not, me bucko."

"And a fine old Irish name it is," Paddy said, giving her as much of a bow as possible while seated.

"That 'tis. Shelaugh as was my ma before me and her ma before her."

"Then Shelaugh, me luv, a beer for me and one for the husband of me beautiful sainted sis." He cupped a hand beside his mouth as if he was trying to keep Dan from hearing. "A married man he is, but I'm free's those goober peanuts over there."

She laughed, then spun on her heel, and headed away, but not before Paddy managed to give her a pat on her well-rounded rump.

She stopped short, turning back to face him, aiming a finger at him as she spoke. "It's for lookin', laddy, not touching, unless you'd be looking to me to shampoo the nits outta the little hair ye got left with that beer you've got comin'."

Paddy self-consciously ran his stubby fingers through his thinning red hair. "Why, if you ain't the sassy one," Paddy said, never losing the crooked grin.

"Sassy ain't the half of it, bucko," she said, spinning on her heel and heading to the bar.

When she returned, carrying a mug in each hand, she hesitated after placing them on the table, and after picking up the pair of dimes Dan had laid there. She glanced back over her shoulder warily before speaking, then did so in a low voice. "So, you'd be Dan McKeag?"

"That I would, lass," Dan said.

"Fellas at the bar are talking about you as if you was already pushing up daisies."

"How so?" Dan asked.

"Saying that there's a couple of fellas down at the end of the bar, the fat-faced one in the narrow-brimmed city hat and the tall, ugly brute in the slouch hat with the porkchop side-whiskers, that have been asking about you, and not in a friendly sort of way. Those boys is pretty well corned, and there's no telling what they'd try and do. They got your name, Mr. McKeag, from another fella at the bar, and I happen to know that those fellas are in town for mischief of some kind."

"Thanks, lass," Dan said, shoving another dime her way.

She picked it up with a thank-you smile, then turned to leave. Dan called her back. "Miss Shelaugh . . ."

"Yes, Mr. McKeag."

"If you should hear more, bring it to me.

If they should start this way, find a fast reason to go out to the necessary."

"Why, Mr. McKeag, I'd be pleased to report back on those louts, and thank you for your concern."

As she moved back to the bar, Paddy reached down and readjusted the muzzle of the shotgun so it aimed more directly at the two at the end of the bar nearest the windows.

The afternoon sun shone through the windows brightly, making it a little hard to see the potential adversaries.

To Dan's surprise, the two men upended their whiskeys and headed for the bat-wing doors. As they did, and Dan carefully watched them, he could hear the hammers on Pad's shotgun ratchet back.

"No problem —" Dan started to say, thinking the men were leaving, as Paddy glanced at him, shrugging his shoulders — but then both the shorter, stocky man in the narrow-brimmed hat and the tall one in the slouch hat spun in a crouch, guns in hand.

"Paddy!" Dan yelled, going for his revolver as a shot splattered into the wall beside his head. Before he could get his weapon palmed and cocked, one barrel of the shotgun roared; then as Dan returned fire, Paddy's other barrel spit flame, but both their adversaries had gotten off at least two shots.

Both men were blown backward by a chest full of buckshot.

The other men in the bar were all on or near the floor, as Dan swept the room with his Remington. But none of them made any move, other than to cower lower. After the reverberating echo of the shots stilled, the only sound in the room was the dragging back of Dan's and Paddy's chairs as they rose and stood, and then Blue barking at the two who were now down and pumping blood. Carefully watching the men in the room, Dan shifted his eyes from man to man, but perceived no threat. Blue stopped his barking, and growled in a quiet rumble at the low moan of one of the two who was still barely alive. The smoke wafting in the ceiling had been added to by the billowing of black powder, and the smell of spent gunpowder hung in the room.

The bartender appeared back over the bar, his eyes wide, as dust motes floated down from the coal-oil chandeliers suspended under the sculpted lead ceiling of the saloon. The afternoon sun reflected off them.

Still, no one made a sound, until the bartender called out. "You fellas blowed a hole in Miss Ballard's front window. She'll be wanting a few dollars for that."

Dan cleared his throat. "Tell Miss Ballard —"

"Tell her yourself," a husky womanly voice called from a doorway at the back of the place. Dan glanced at the woman as she stepped into the room, then turned his attention to her. She ignored the two men with guns still palmed for a moment, walked over and had a short, low conversation with the bartender, then turned back to Dan and Pad.

"Miss Ballard, I presume," Dan said, tipping his hat, "you should have a better sort of customer in your place. Your window would not suffer a hole if you did." She eyed Dan, and the dog that had crossed the room to stand at his side.

"Window didn't shoot a hole in itself," she said.

Dan was not prone to argue with a beautiful woman, and the woman called Miss Ballard was certainly that, with auburn hair to her waist, its curls resting on a bustled dress the hem of which brushed the floor and the neck of which was buttoned at the throat. Eyes the color of a clear summer sky appraised him carefully. Her complexion had a single dark blemish — Dan thought the mark, just on her left cheekbone, was applied with a grease pencil.

While Dan eyed her, so much so a tinge of guilt crossed his mind as he'd left his own beautiful wife, Erin, along with his young nephew and five hired hands, to watch the Lucky Seven, Paddy crossed the room and poked at the two men with the barrel of the shotgun.

"The old man in the black frock coat done put his brand on both of these boys," he said quietly.

One of them had died sitting upright against the front wall of the saloon, just under the holed window; the other was splayed out beneath the bat-wing doors, still moaning softly. Paddy noted that both had a smattering of buckshot in their chests, but the one leaning against the wall had the added insult of a .44 hole in his forehead just under the brim of the bowler hat he still wore.

The woman momentarily turned her attention to the bar, speaking to a slightly rotund man in a city suit and four-in-hand tie. "Doc, you gonna take a look at that one that's still moaning?"

"That boy's got a dozen or two holes in his chest, Rose. It'd be a waste of good drinkin' time. He'll stop his complaining in a minute or two."

She turned her attention back to McKeag. She was a patient woman, and said nothing, looking expectantly, waiting for Dan to respond.

Finally, he gave her a tight smile. "And just how many dollars would that window be costin'?"

"A dollar for the glass, and a dollar for the glazier to install it."

"And it seems there a hole in your wall, about an inch from where my head was," Dan added.

"I imagine one of those fellows who've bloodied up my floor has a dollar in his pocket to cover the cost of hanging another roll of paper . . . particularly since your good looks were almost spread all over my wall."

"Thank you for the compliment. You're not only a handsome but a fair woman, Miss Ballard, so here's your two dollars." Dan dug in his pocket for a couple of coins with his free hand. As he was handing them to her, the bat-wing doors crashed open, the entrants having to leap over the man lying there. Dan stepped in front of

29

the woman, shoving her behind, shielding her from the threat, as two men filled the doorway while Dan filled his hand with the revolver he'd holstered.

"Don't shoot," she yelled in his ear. "It's the law."

Chapter 3

Both intruders had on city suits, with their coats pulled back so their copper badges pinned to their waistcoats were clearly in view, and both were armed, with Bulldog revolvers in hand.

Blue began a deep growl, but Dan hushed him, telling him to lie down. The dog did, but it was obvious he was not happy about it.

Dan could see little more than their silhouettes with the sun behind them. Had the woman not yelled out, he would likely have killed a lawman.

He lowered his revolver. It was obvious they both knew Paddy Dundee well, as one of them walked over and took the shotgun out of his hands without getting a protest from the ex-bank guard.

"You," one of them shouted to McKeag, "grab that Remington by the barrel and bring it over here."

Dan sighed deeply. The last thing he wanted with five more hired killers still looking for him was to give up his .44-40 Remington. But he also didn't need the law against him . . . it seemed he had plenty else to worry about at the moment.

He reversed the big revolver in his hand, again instructed Blue to hush and lie down, then walked over and handed the revolver to a barrel-chested deputy, butt first.

"You'll be turning around so I can put the irons on you," the man said.

"The hell you say," Paddy Dundee interrupted, limping forward, shoving his way between the deputy and Dan.

"You'll be going to jail," the deputy said, "until there's a hearing . . . the both of you. Those two fellas on the floor have so much lead in them, we ought to melt them down for bullets."

Blue couldn't stand it, and barked, then moved slowly across the room toward the deputies, the hair on his back on end.

"Blue, get over there and lie down," Dan snapped, and the dog moved back, but still growled a low rumble.

The lady, who apparently owned the place, stepped forward. "Howard. These gentlemen were sitting peacefully at their table, having a drink, when those two on the floor started firing at them. They fired back in self-defense."

"That's right . . . just how it happened," the barmaid, Shelaugh, offered, stepping out from where she'd taken shelter behind the bar.

Miss Ballard turned toward the bar, where several men leaned, watching the scene with interest as it unfolded. "Paul?" she called out.

The bartender stepped away so as to be clearly seen by the deputies. "That's right. Those two had just got their beers, and was mindin' their own business . . . peaceful as Sunday morning."

"Doc?" she said to the rotund man in four-in-hand.

"Clearly in self-defense. Hell's bells, those two louts got off at least two shots — never a word said — before these two fellas even knew what was happening."

"Still and all —" the big deputy started to complain, but was silenced by the woman.

"No still and all about it, Howard Perkins. You'll not be taking these fellas out of my place for legitimately defending themselves. The law gives us all that right."

"Rose, you're not the law here in Helena," the deputy snapped.

"And you're a long ways from the last word in the law here in Helena. Go fetch

Judge Harley or the marshal if you want to find out I'm right."

"I'll be taking these fellas —"

"Bull, Howard." She stepped up right in his face. "Go fetch one of them. I'll watch over these fellows and they'll be here when you get back. You know Pad Dundee well, and can find him at the bank damn near anytime —" Pad didn't correct her, under the circumstances — "and you are?"

"Dan McKeag. I ranch twelve thousand acres over near Deer Lodge City."

"Then," she continued, "Mr. McKeag will not be hard to find. I'd already taken a larruping dislike for those two there on the floor . . . they won't be waking up in the great beyond sportin' halos. Filthy-mouthed and disrespectful they were, and I should have thrown them out days ago. By the way, drag them out on your way. They're smelling up my place."

The deputy reddened, but handed Dan's revolver back to him, then did as he was told, bending and grabbing the shorter of the two attackers by the collar and dragging him along as he left. The other deputy dragged the taller one out in the street, where the two deputies left them before they walked off.

"Much obliged," Dan said, tipping his

hat to the woman, who extended her hand.

"I'm Rose Ballard, and this is my place, and I'm going to break a longtime rule and buy you fellows a drink before I go back to my books." She turned her attention to the swamper. "Toby, get your mop to that awful mess . . . there's blood and bone splinters all over my wall and floor."

"Obliged for the drink offer," Dan said, "but it's me who should be doing the buying."

"Then I don't have to break my own rule," she said, flashing him a smile that sent a bolt of heat down his backbone.

Paddy stopped the old swamper on his way by. "I fancy that ol' boy's bowler hat, Pop. Fetch it for me if you would. It'll be a good trade for the pair of shotgun loads those louts cost me."

Rose Ballard gave the swamper a nod.

"Yes, sir," the old man said, and hurried over to the mess with his mop and bucket.

"You'd be a cold one, Paddy Dundee, cold as a banker's heart," Rose said as they took a seat at the same corner table.

"No, ma'am. Neither am I a wasteful one. Man shouldn't go to meet his maker with a hat on nohow, and it's a fair trade. Not that either of those two will spend much time beggin' at St. Peter's gate afore they're sidetracked to hell."

She nodded at the men just outside her door. "Doubt if they'd agree, if they were still in the agreeing stage." She turned her attention to Dan. "So, Mr. McKeag, what brings you to Helena?"

"Had a visit with the bank, and come to find out there's those two and a handful more been paid to clear the way for Bert Prager to buy . . . or steal . . . my ranch."

"And just how are they to do that?"

"Well, it seems that I'm the major impediment to the transaction."

"So why not just sell out?"

"Never."

"Then am I to expect more holes in my windows and walls?"

"No, ma'am. As soon as I finish another of those fine cool beers of yours, we'll be moving on."

"It's been a pleasure knowing you, Mr. McKeag." She rose to her feet.

"You're not going to let me buy you that drink?" Dan said, standing also.

"No, I've got figures to do, and what I drink muddies the mind and I should have a clear head. But I'll let you owe me one."

"My pleasure."

She started for the rear door, then

stopped and turned back. "I thank you for looking out for me, Mr. McKeag."

"How so?" Dan asked.

"You stepped in front of me when those lawmen slammed my doors dang near off their hinges. Don't think I didn't notice."

"Better my old ugly hide ventilated than your fine fair one."

She smiled again. "Not so old, I'd say, Mr. McKeag, and not all that ugly. I wish you well."

"It might take more than wishes, but I appreciate it." He studied her carefully as he spoke again. "Their dying in your place . . . you seemed to take it well?"

She eyed him carefully, then slightly shook her head. "Mr. McKeag, running a place like the Bonny Glen will thicken one's hide, fair or not."

She nodded, then disappeared into the rear.

"Damn fine-lookin' woman," Paddy said, staring after her. Then he turned his attention to the bowler the swamper had brought him. He fitted it on his head and it dropped to his ears, folding the cauliflowered one a little. "Damn, gonna need some paper lining."

"An understatement, Paddy my lad. A true understatement."

"What? Paper lining?"

"The woman. She's more than merely fine-looking."

"You're married tight as a well-fitted horseshoe and hoof, Dan McKeag," Paddy scolded, then guffawed.

They finished their beers, and were heading for the door with Blue pacing them closely, when the bat-wings swung aside again. Blue growled, but Dan laid a hand on his head and the big dog quieted. This man also sported a copper badge on his waistcoat, and the two deputies were close behind.

"Paddy." The man tipped his broad-brimmed hat. He wore a city suit, but over boots and under a drover's wide-brimmed hat.

"Dan McKeag," Paddy said, "this is Territorial Federal Marshal Harbin Smyth."

Dan extended his hand, and the marshal took it but quickly asked, "That mess outside your work?"

"It's not my vocation, nor my avocation, Marshal, just something I was forced to do . . . if I didn't want to be the one in the dirt."

"Humph," he said. "The rumor was you had trouble waiting for you here in Helena.

We don't abide by that sort of thing here. Don't leave town until I get to the bottom of all this."

"I didn't bring any trouble to your town, Marshal — that would be Bert Prager's doin' — but I don't run from it either. And I'm not planning on going anywhere until tomorrow at first light."

"And you're staying where?"

"The Palace. Room 320. If you don't mind, Pad and I will head there now, and I will be there for supper and overnight."

"You're the Dan McKeag from over Deer Lodge City way — the Lucky Seven McKeag?"

"One and the same."

"Then you won't be hard to find. Try and keep that hogleg holstered, Mr. McKeag."

"So long as I don't run into any more Helena visitors with mischief on their minds." With that, Dan tipped his hat and headed out, with Paddy close behind.

They turned back toward the main part of town and the three-story hotel.

Just as they reached the corner of the Bonny Glen, there was a six-foot-wide space between it and the Miner's supply store next door.

A small voice called out as they passed. "Mr. McKeag."

Warily, Dan looked down the shaded lane between the buildings, surprised to see the barmaid, Shelaugh, in the shadows. He said to Pad over his shoulder, "Keep a sharp eye. I'm going to see what she wants. Blue, stay. Stay with Pad."

Pad scratched the big dog's ears. "I'm going to saunter down the street a ways and check things out. Come on, Blue."

Dan strode a half-dozen paces into the weed-covered passageway. The bargirl stood with hands folded behind her back, looking worried.

"I've heard a bit more," she said, a tight smile on her face.

"And that is?" Dan asked.

She smiled fetchingly. "That is going to be costing you a dollar, Mr. McKeag."

Dan sighed, but dug into his pocket with his right hand.

To his great surprise, with his gun hand deep in the pocket fumbling for a dollar, she raised a stubby .31 Colt Pocket Model, already cocked, and almost before he could comprehend, it spit flame and the fires of perdition filled his chest.

He was slammed back, staggering, and then, as he was trying to clear his head, he heard her cock it again, then the report of the gun before the echo of the first shot had left the alley, and he was flat on his back, staring up at the narrow slit of sky between the buildings.

You're a damn fool, Dan McKeag, he thought, *you're going to wake up with candles around the bed,* clutching his chest as pain enveloped him, then all thought and feeling faded.

Paddy Dundee palmed his revolver and, with Blue following, ran into the passageway in time to see the red and black dress disappear around the corner in the distance, and to find Dan spread-eagled on the ground, his life's blood soaking into the dirt.

"Dan, Dan!" he called out, but didn't even get a twitch in response. He quickly searched the rooflines and ridge behind the buildings for the shooter, but whoever the blackguard was, was nowhere to be seen. Maybe the woman had seen him?

Blue sniffed at his prostrate unmoving master, then sat on his haunches and began to whine, then to howl. A deep keening cry to let the world know his life had suddenly gone terribly wrong.

Paddy kneeled beside Dan. "Dan," he said again quietly. Then his voice caught and his throat began to burn and eyes dampen as words wouldn't come. He

41

couldn't help but think of his hardheaded-
ness for the past eight years, and how that
had kept him from staying friends with this
man. All he could do was *think* what he'd
been about to say, for his throat was so
knotted he couldn't have spoken it. As the
dog continued to wail, he bowed his head
and thought, *Dan McKeag, may your soul
be in heaven an hour before the devil
knows you're dead.*

Chapter 4

"Where is the bastard?" Bert Prager demanded, then spit a stream of tobacco juice into the cuspidor at the chair's side.

He sat in his hotel room, five men and a woman standing in front of him.

"They carried him into the rear of the Bonny Glen," said one of men, known only as Brownie. "He was dead as a smoked ham." Brownie was by far the largest of the four men, filling the doorway when he passed through.

"I ain't paying until I see him laid out," Prager said.

The woman, still dressed in the black-and-red gown and net stockings she'd worn to work, stepped forward. "The deal was five hundred, and it's the five hundred you promised that Brownie and I want, and we want it now, Mr. Prager."

He didn't even look at the woman, but rather glared at the man called Brownie. "Didn't figure on you using no split-tail to do a man's work."

Brownie guffawed. "You wanted him dead, and you didn't say how. In fact, you said you didn't give a *damn* how. Shelaugh and I are a team, and she's a fair shot, as you now know, particularly as the men don't mind getting close up to her. Thompson and Willard tried the old boy on and they're both dead as salted cod. It took Shelaugh here to finish the job. McKeag's dead. You'll be wantin' us out of town before the law comes callin'. Pay up."

About that time, a rap on the door echoed, and Prager walked over and flung it open.

"Mr. Prager." It was the thick-chested marshal's deputy, Howard Perkins. "I just talked to the undertaker, and McKeag is laid out cold as a stone. Old Smithers is building McKeag's box now, and they plan to haul him back to Deer Lodge on tomorrow's freight wagon so his widder woman can come fetch him."

"Tell Smithers that's not going to happen. I don't want no ghost of a McKeag haunting my new ranch. Bury him here or feed him to the damn hogs . . . I couldn't care less." He dug in his pocket and pulled out a ten-dollar gold piece. "Take this to Smithers," Prager said, "and tell him McKeag is to be planted here. It's my pleasure to foot the bill."

"But his wife will want . . ."

"His wife will . . . will be on the train east soon after I get back to Deer Lodge City. Do as I say."

"Yes, sir," the deputy said, and stalked out, the ten-dollar gold piece grasped tightly in a big fist.

Prager hobbled to a fold-down desk against the wall, and scribbled on a sheet of paper. When done, he waved Brownie over. He wanted no trouble from this huge man, who might get to you and rip your head off with his bare hands, even if you put a slug in the middle of his broad chest. "Here's a draft, made out to you. Take it to Silas Bingham at the Stookmen and Merchants Bank. He'll give you your five hundred; then I don't ever want to see you again. In fact, you and your woman be on the stage in the morning." He gave the two of them the hardest look he could muster, and added, "I suggest you head for Oregon or California. Don't let me hear you're in Montana after the time it takes you to get the hell out."

Brownie tipped his narrow-brimmed hat, and he and the woman were out the door.

Prager hobbled back to the desk, pulled

open a drawer, fidgeted a minute, then turned to the others. "Outdone by a woman! Two bad McKeag didn't shoot the lot of you before the woman got to him. Would have saved me a handful of fifty-dollar gold pieces . . ." Disgusted, Prager handed ten to each of the four remaining rough-looking men, then paused and eyed them. "I'm paying you for this piece of work 'cause I'm an honorable man." He eyed each of them in turn, making sure none of them snickered at that, then continued. "There's more to do here. There's the matter of a half-dozen hired hands on the Lucky Seven — most of them too stupid to go to work for the Bar X. They might go peaceable; then again, some of them seem to pay mind to the McKeag missus. They all got to join up or go, one way or the other. There's another five fifty-dollar gold pieces in it for any of you who'll take on the job of cleaning out that rat's nest so I get no trouble there. Can you boys ride for the brand?"

Each of them nodded his head.

"I'll be going back to the ranch in my buggy tomorrow. Y'all need to ride out soon as you can get provisioned and saddled up. Take a couple of boxes of cartridges each. Them McKeag hands might take some urging to get them to leave. Meet me at the Bar X in three days."

After they left, Prager hobbled over to a side table that held a glass, a bone-white basin and a pitcher of water, and a lone bottle of Baughman's Black Silk Whiskey. He poured himself three fingers of the brew, toasted the polished metal mirror hanging above the basin, smiled at his reflection, and offered, "To you, Bert Prager, and your new ranch. Now the Lucky Seven is no more, and the Bar X is twelve thousand acres more grand. Here's to thirty-three thousand acres of fine Montana grass and timber . . . and so much more."

If Prager were the kind inclined to, and if he could have done a jig with his bum leg, he would have.

Instead, he upended the glass.

But he didn't have but one, for he had one more piece of business to attend to before he left town. Judge Oscar Pettibone Harley.

When Shelaugh and Brownie were out of the hotel, Brownie glanced over at her. "How did Thompson and that fat Georgia boy —"

"Willard."

"Thompson and Willard . . . how'd they

go and get themselves laid out toes up?"

"I warned McKeag and that bank guard, that's how."

He stopped her on the boardwalk, turning her to face him. "You did what?"

She'd let her hair down, and twirled a strand in her hand as she batted her eyes at him. "Brownie, it's too bad your brain ain't as big as the rest of you . . . would we be having a pocket fulla money if'n *they'd* shot McKeag?"

"No . . . I guess we wouldn't."

"Did you owe those two highbinders a damned thing?"

"Nope."

"Then I did right, didn't I?"

Brownie took a deep breath, then shook his head. "Yeah, I guess you are right. Still and all, it don't seem proper —"

"Are your pockets full?"

When he had no answer, she continued. "Let's get to the room so I can get this fancy dress off and get my riding skirt on. Let's see if we can make Hell Gate in three or four days. I hear there's a fine French seamstress there, and you can afford to buy me three or four new dresses . . . with matching parasols and reticules."

He shrugged, and they turned and headed for their room to pack.

★ ★ ★

Erin McKeag sat, dressed in gingham and ready for work, before a polished mirror in the bedroom of Lucky Seven's small log ranch house, brushing waist-long sandy hair that draped over her shoulder in front of her down across her breasts. She never seemed to have time to give her hair the hundred strokes per handful — that had been her childhood habit — when Dan was there, and now she was indulging herself. Her green eyes had fine lines at the corners and a hint of darkness under them, and she sighed deeply as she worked night-time kinks out of fine long locks. She hadn't slept well, tossing and turning . . . but then she never did when Dan was gone.

Dan had been gone a full ten days — this was actually the eleventh morning — had promised to be home several nights ago — two hard days' ride there, two in town, and two hard days' ride home. She was beginning to really worry.

But she knew worrying was foolish, although it seemed a woman's lot in life. Oftentimes when Dan was gone, worry niggled at her, but this time it was a heavy stone nestled in the bottom of her stomach.

The little ranch house had only one bedroom, and Erin hoped — prayed — that they would soon have reason to add another. She was three weeks late with her monthly, and they'd been trying for the eight years they'd been married to have a child, children, but so far to no avail. The devil of it was, she'd been with child when they married, but she'd lost it not long after they arrived at the ranch.

Please, God, let this be the time, she thought, but a quiet knock on the door turned her attention back to what busied her while Dan was gone — the day-to-day operation of the Lucky Seven.

She rose, walked to the door, and opened it.

"Mornin', Aunt Erin," her nephew said with his normal wide grin, handing her a steaming mug of coffee, black and rich as melted tar. "Cookie's got biscuits and elk sausage 'bout ready. You want to come to the bunkhouse and join the boys. You're invited!"

She couldn't help but catch the infection of the boy's grin. At fourteen, Roan was big for his age, his height equal to hers. He had the good looks of the McKeags, with coal-black hair, shining blue eyes, and a black-Irish-smooth rosy-cheeked complexion, but he was all gangly arms and legs, still clumsy as a month-old hound pup.

"I would love to," she said quickly, then admitted, "It's a bit lonely in the house with Dan gone." She twirled a long strand of hair between her fingers. "Let me tie this mop up and I'll be right along."

Roan slapped his thigh and turned to head for the door, catching a toe on the main room's hoop rug. Stopping to straighten it, he gave her a slightly embarrassed look back over his shoulder, then continued out.

In moments she stood at the bunkhouse door, her long hair rolled in a bun behind her head, and knocked quietly.

Simon Coppersmith opened the door, stepped back, trying to arrange his large bulk so she could pass, and puffed out his chest as if she were royalty. Her nephew and four other men rose from their spots at the long plank table, removing their hats in the same motion. She entered, a quart of huckleberry jam in hand. She strolled over and placed it in the center of the table to the smiles of the men.

"We're proud you joined us," Simon said, closing the door behind her, then hurrying over to pull out a chair at the head of the table. The hands waited until she was seated, then settled down themselves.

Most ranch women were expected to cook for family and hands, but that had never been the case at the Lucky Seven. Simon, a big barrel-chested man with a full salt-and-pepper beard, had been the ranch cook long before Erin arrived, and had seemed, at least to Erin, quietly crushed at the thought she would be taking over his pot-and-pan chores. But Dan was adamant; he wanted the two of them, the newlyweds, to eat in the house, together, at least two meals a day. They were occasionally joined by Roan, but he bunked with and normally ate with the hands. Simon had been relieved to retain his favorite chore — feeding the hands.

Simon also did the blacksmithing and tended the tack, so it wasn't as if he'd be out of work had she taken over the cooking chores, but he was proud of his work, and she was happy for her privacy in the ranch house.

Besides, Simon was a fine camp cook.

It was somewhat of a treat for her to be served and eat with the hands, on rare occasion.

She liked the men — had never been really comfortable around other women, except for Meegan Dugan and Anne Greenlaw — and felt men liked her, even though they couldn't scratch and spit when she was a guest in the bunkhouse.

Simon — Cookie, as he was known to the men — returned to his stove, then glanced back at her. "I've got a couple of hen's eggs, Missy, if you'd care for them?"

"I'll eat what the men eat, thank you, Simon."

He nodded, smiled knowingly, poured her a cup and brought it to her, then returned to his oven and pulled out a pan of well-browned biscuits.

They were dropped in the center of the table, and he quickly set a cast-iron skillet full of flour gravy on one side of them and a heaping platter of elk sausage on the other. Then he added a ladle to the skillet's contents, and a serving fork to the sausage platter. Roan, sitting to Erin's right, picked out two fat biscuits, caught Cookie's hard stare, then redeemed himself by placing them carefully on Erin's plate.

"You want gravy?" Roan asked.

She split one of the biscuits. "On that one, please. I'll save the other for the jam."

He took her plate to the skillet, rather than trying to bring the hot skillet to her place, and dipped out a generous ladle full

53

of gravy, then passed it back to her.

Tennessee Tom Macklin, Poker Pete Howard, Slim John Scroggins, and Skeeter McKelvie filled the rest of the ladder-back chairs at the table. Cookie took a seat at the far end, facing Erin.

No one made a move to fill their own plate, nor did Erin pick up a fork, until Cookie took his seat, then bowed his head. He mouthed a quick grace, and the men waited respectfully with heads lowered and eyes closed as he did. More than one of them had received a crack across the head with spatula or serving spoon when they were new to the outfit and had taken a bite before the grace was given; but as if a starter's pistol had been fired, when Cookie mouthed "Amen," they dug in and it was every hand for himself.

Plates covered with three palm-sized split biscuits, overlapping, were smothered in gravy and topped with patties of elk sausage. A pitcher of coffee was passed, as well as a pitcher of fresh-churned buttermilk.

Skeeter McKelvie had gotten the nickname because he was about the size of one — the only man at the table smaller than even Roan. But he was all rawhide, sinew, and spring-steel. With his mouth full of biscuits and gravy, he asked her, "When's the boss due back?"

"Way past due," she said with a worried look, and he was sorry he asked.

"It's a long haul, Missy," Cookie said. "Don't you be worrying about Dan McKeag. He's been through hell, pardon the term, ma'am . . . and high water, and if any man can take care of himself, it's Dan McKeag."

Chapter 5

Erin McKeag smiled at Cookie's reassurance. "I'm sure he'll come dragging in today, full of vinegar and refusing to admit he's dead tired, and full of questions for all of you."

The men laughed, knowing that each of them had been assigned a dozen tasks before Dan had ridden out, and knowing they damned well better have finished them before he returned — which they all had days before.

Tennessee Tom was the hand longest riding for the brand, the Lucky Seven. He'd gone to work for Dan's dad well before Dan could remember, and if there was a ramrod, a number-two man, it was Tom. He was black as a bat cave, with tight gray hair, and had ridden in on a tall skunk-striped dun mule well before the War Between the States, when the Lucky Seven was nothing but a timber shack on a frontier that most hadn't even heard of — a shack that now served as smokehouse. The oldest of four buildings on the ranch.

Dan's father, Fletcher, had never bothered to ask Tennessee how he'd come to choose Montana — or if he was an escaped slave, which was what the old man suspected — when Tennessee asked for work, or at least for a place to sleep out the storm that was howling across the land. When old Fletcher McKeag, with a wife dead of the fever and a pair of young sons to raise, watched Tom's mule back up, spin on a dime, and follow voice commands, he offered the hulking black man a bunk and found to stay on. Fletcher had a growing string of horses, in addition to the few cattle he had then, and he needed a man good with that critter to break and train. It had only been a couple of years since Fletcher had turned his attention from wolfing and trapping, at which his father before him had made a living. Sean, the first McKeag on McKeag's Mountain, had been pure trapper and hunter.

Tennessee Tom had been on the place ever since, had been a second father to Dan, and was now filling that job for Roan.

Dan had taken Roan in when the boy was but seven, only three years after he'd married Erin. The boy's father, Tobin, and mother, older brother, and sister had been killed by the Blackfoot Indians while moving north, working their way across the plains to Benton's Fort with a load of furs. Roan had only stayed alive by remaining dead-still and silent under a dozen wolf skins, then escaping the wagon in the dead of night after the hunting party of braves had partaken of Tobin's jug until stupefied.

It had taken the boy a week, riding one of the team horses with a hackamore tied from a lead rope, to find his way to McKeag's Mountain and his uncle. But he did, managing to stay alive at that young age across some tough country with nothing but berries, tule root, and a single slingshot-slain grouse to eat.

He hadn't spoken for almost a month after he arrived, only nodding or shaking his head when questioned about his family. Slowly, Dan and Tom brought him around, but he still didn't laugh as much as most young people.

While Erin helped Cookie clean up, the men discussed the day's work. There was a deep gorge on the north side of the mountain, a rough place of rock faces and flats, steps thick with lodgepole pine that a man could barely walk through, much less horseback.

Tennessee Tom thought there were a number of wild cows and their calves holed up in the gorge, and he wanted the men to drive it from top to bottom and see what they could push out.

"Ain't no damned cows in that mess," Slim John Scroggins stated, as if it were gospel from the Mount.

"Oh," Tom said, "you ride that rough ground lately, Slim John?"

The thin-faced man, who was the latest addition to the Lucky Seven crew, looked up from his coffee cup. "Ain't never rid it, but I can tell you, dumb as cows is, they ain't in that pile of rocks."

Tom took a deep breath. He hadn't liked the man since Dan had hired him the fall before when they'd needed hands to drive the cattle down from the high country. His patience was beginning to wear fine as frog's hair with Slim Scroggins, but as patiently as possible he said, "I don't imagine you'd be so kind as to indulge the rest of us and join us in a saunter down that old canyon?"

Slim looked, and sounded, disgusted, but downed the rest of his coffee and said, "You're the boss around here."

"Glad you noticed," Tom said, rising and stretching. "Well, best we pound the kinks outta our critters. The mountain ain't getting any smaller, and we're kickin' daylight behind us."

"That mule you ride," Slim said, his tone even more disgusted than it had been, "ain't fittin' to be called a critter. He's nothing but a freak of nature."

"We'll see who gets down the mountain without skinnin' his butt — pardon me, ma'am — his backside," Tennessee said, turning his attention to Erin. She nodded with a grin. Tom turned back to the sallow-faced Slim Scroggins. "In fact, I'll be happy to race that old mule against that sorry sorrel you ride for, say — a ten-dollar gold piece, any time you say." He glanced at Erin, then added, "When we're on our own time, of course."

"Ha," Slim said with a low cackle. "How about come Sunday. A quarter mile from a standing start."

"Ha yerself," Tennessee said. "Five miles from here to the top of the mountain, or from the top of the mountain down . . . your choice."

"No bet," Slim said, heading for the door. He knew his shallow-chested sorrel, fast as he was for a short distance, would never outlast Tom's mule. He slammed the door behind him with no further comment.

"Ya'll gonna be back in time for a seven o'clock supper?" Cookie asked, handing

Tom a canvas sack full of cold grub —
jerky, hardtack, and some canned peaches
— for the drive down the mountain.

"Doubt it," Tom said. "It's four hours'
hard ride up there, then more down the
tough side, particularly if we pick up some
beeves to drive. Leave the beans on . . . if
that's to your liking?"

Even Tom was careful with Cookie's
feelings and supper plans. It didn't pay to
be on the bad side of the man with the
spatula.

Tom hoisted the sack over his shoulder
and headed for the door. "Let's get some
leather on 'em and get up the mountain.
The sun's on the prod."

High on a ridge overlooking the ranch
house, four men sat or stood near their
horses. They'd ridden hard from Helena to
reach the Prager ranch, the Bar X, beating
Old Man Prager there by several hours.
And it was a good thing, as the old man
hadn't been at his place more than an hour
before he had them mounted and ready to
ride again.

They'd covered the fifteen miles to the
McKeag place before sundown, then spent
a long night in a cold camp overlooking the
Lucky Seven. Come dawn, they had

counted six men on the place, plus the woman. They'd palavered after being satisfied that seven were all there were, deciding that if the hands all stayed at the home place, their job would be much more difficult. But if the hands set out to different parts of the ranch for chores, then they'd be easy pickings.

Badger Hotchkins was not the tallest of the four, but was reputed to be the toughest man ever to ride up out of Colorado. He was wide though the shoulders, with long powerful arms, short stubby legs, a hooded brow that gave him a primitive look, and a chest thick as a tree stump. Dark hair hung over his eyes, and he was never clean-shaven, using only a big knife on his hair and beard when it got over the two inches he preferred to keep it. Its shagginess gave him a perpetual wild look. Badger didn't talk much, but when he did the others listened.

Badger centered his eyes on the sandy-blond man with an ugly y-shaped scar on his left cheek. "Al, I want you and Blodget to ride round the ranch without bein' seen and take up on that far ridge just inside the tree line."

Alvin Givens scratched heavy porkchop sideburns and eyed the shorter man, wondering who'd made him boss of this outfit, but since Badger sat his horse only an arm's length away with an Arkansas whetstone in one hand, stropping the big knife he usually wore on his hip, he decided it was best not to broach the subject at the moment.

"So where will you and Slater be . . . waitin' here for a chance at the woman?"

Badger gave him a hard look, and held the big knife out, using it as a pointer. "You do as I say, or I'll scar the other cheek to match the ugly one . . . and we'll finish this and be on our way afore nightfall."

"I doubt that," Al mumbled, but flinched away when Badger poked him with the big blade, and quickly added, "You want we should stay away from the house?"

"We'll all stay away, and like we said, we'll pick them off one at a time." Badger flashed a yellow-toothed grin at the rest of them. "You go at a man with a big smile on yer face and he don't know he's dead until he's got a mouth fulla gravel. When we got it down to two or three left, then we'll ride on the house, when it's nothin' but the woman and the cook."

"Prager said that ol' boy, Coppersmith I

believe he said — he ain't yer normal cook. Coppersmith was a blacksmith in town afore he come out here, and a fightin' man in the war before that. He may have more than a bean spoon or tongs in hand. . . ."

"You two ride on out. Let me do the thinkin'."

"Come on, Slater," Badger yelled back to a tall, gaunt man dressed like a gambler in black trousers and stripped frock coat who was finishing up saddling his seventeen-hand dappled gray horse. He would have been a handsome man if it weren't for a crooked eye that made you wonder which one was watching you.

"What?" he said.

"We're splittin' up — you and me is riding over across the way."

Badger snapped at the other two. "And don't be firin' your weapons lessen you have to. If any ride out your way, smile like a long-lost relative, then club 'em down and slit their gullets, so as you don't warn the rest of them."

Slater eyed him, with his bad eye closed, for a long moment before he poked a stirrup with a pointed black boot and swung up in the saddle of his tall gray, then said in a low voice, "Prager said we should ask 'em if they wanted to go to work for the Bar X, and only shoot 'em down if they don't. And the woman and boy was to have the chance to ride out and go east."

"And I say why bother. Leave 'em all for the buzzards and it'll be a lot less trouble."

Slater merely shrugged, then slipped his revolver from its greased holster, spun the cylinder, and checked its loads. "Don't make no never mind to me either way. Pay's the same."

"Then let's get to it," Badger growled, and they reined away.

Chapter 6

The big cow dog, Blue, lay at the end of the bed, his light gray eyes following the woman, Rose Ballard, as she crossed the room. Paddy Dundee sat in a rocker, slowly moving, just enough to make it squeak.

"Any change?" she asked, handing Paddy a mug of tea.

"He moaned a little a minute ago."

"That's better than that ghastly shallow breathing, waiting for each one to be his last."

"Soup."

The voice mouthing the whispered word was so distant and faint both of them stopped moving, just to listen.

"What?" Rose finally said.

"Soup," he said again, slightly louder, drawing the word out like a moan.

Both Rose and Paddy laughed aloud, and hurried to the bedside.

"What's funny?" he managed weakly, his eyes only slits in a gaunt sallow face.

"You're awake," Paddy said, trying to

keep his voice from cracking.

"Hungry . . . something wet," he whispered.

"I'll go make some soup," Rose said, a wide smile on her face.

Paddy fetched a glass off a side table and poured it full from a bone pitcher, then returned to the bed and lifted Dan's head enough so he could drink. He took only a few sips, then managed to wave Paddy away.

"I feel half kilt," Dan whispered, his eyes only partway open.

"Three quarters maybe. Thought you was all kilt for a while there," Pad said. "Then if'n you was kilt you wouldn't feel nothing, so be thankful. You took two in the chest. Doc dug one out, but said the other had to stay. Any reasonable man woulda went on to meet his maker and not caused all this trouble."

"How long?" Dan asked.

"You been in Miss Rose's bed for the better part of a week, with her and me taking turns sleepin' in the sitting room, when she wasn't workin' downstairs. We been pourin' water and broth down your gullet, but you ain't had much."

"Erin?"

"I sent a telegram, but ain't seen hide

nor hair of her. I couldn't tell her you was shot and still breathing 'cause I don't trust that skinny Wilbur Prichard over at the Western Union not to mouth it about. I just told her to come quick."

"She'll come."

"You rest now. Rose will be up with some soup. Doc Gallagher said if you woke up, you'd make it, but you'll take some mendin'."

"Prager?"

"No one knows you're here but Rose, Doc, and me . . . and the digger, but I paid him well to keep his mouth shut — with your money, of course. The swamper, Toby, knows too, but Rose said his mouth is tight as a tick in a lamb's tail. We done had your funeral and buried a box of rocks a few days ago. Said you was shot up so bad you wouldn't want folks to see you. Closed coffin it was . . . though most folks wouldn't of known the difference 'twixt you and a pile of rocks. Figured you didn't want to pay for no fancy headstone, so it's only a cheap wood cross."

A slight smile crossed Dan's lips. "Was it a good funeral?"

"Well attended, Danny boy. Half the folks in town . . . course I sponsored the wake with your gold coin, and most of the mourners was the town drunks who only cried when I stopped buyin'. Held it right downstairs in the Bonny Glen, and a fine shindig it was, with many a toast to yer memory. Now you rest."

"Dancer?" Dan was worried about his blood stud.

"He's in the livery, well tended."

"Blue?"

Before Paddy could answer, hearing his name, the dog was at the bedside, laying his big head on Dan's hand. Dan managed to raise it enough to scratch the dog's ears. Then his hand relaxed, and Paddy realized he'd fallen asleep.

But Paddy had a smile on his face for the first time in more than a week.

He returned to his rocker, and Blue to the hoop rug at the foot of the bed, following his tail a couple of rounds before he flopped down.

As Pad rocked, he couldn't help but again lament at the fool he'd been the last few years. Dan McKeag had come to him to ask for his little sister's hand in marriage. It wasn't as if Pad and Erin didn't have a pa, but their ma and da were still in County Kildare. Pad insisted that he write the old man and get his blessing on the union, but Dan McKeag was not about to wait for the post to Ireland and back. He'd insisted that Pad give the permission. Pad was incensed when he found that they'd gone to the preacher without his, or his da's, blessing. It was years later when Erin had confessed to him that she'd been with child — a child she'd lost to miscarriage — and waiting was out of the question.

By that time, Pad was so used to the feud with Dan McKeag that neither of them knew how to stop it and still save face. Pad knew that Dan was a man who'd stood on his hind legs long before he was weaned, was all heart above his belly button and guts below, and didn't have much paw and beller to him. He wasn't the talkative kind. It might have been another eight years before they forgot what they were arguing about, had it not been for a half-dozen hired killers.

It was the word that seven hired guns were in town being paid to kill his sister's husband that had finally turned the trick.

Blood is even thicker than pride.

Givens and Blodget had only been gone for a few minutes when Badger saw in the distance the bunkhouse emptying out. Far below, five hands headed for the barn, then in moments rode out toward the mountain.

"Damn the flies," Badger mumbled. "They're all riding out together."

Slater walked over beside him and looked down at the cluster of buildings in the valley bottom. "Let's pace them and see what they're up to. Maybe we can pick them off one at a time."

"That's good as any."

They tightened their cinches, mounted, and set a course that would parallel that of the Lucky Seven hands.

Givens and Blodget were at the upper end of the valley, crossing Spotted Dog Creek, when they saw the riders set out from the ranch complex.

"Let's get up in them trees," Givens said, gigging his horse into a trot. Blodget paced him close behind.

They worked their way up into a stand of fir, then reined around.

"Hell's bells," Blodget said. "They're all riding out together. This ain't fittin' with Badger's plan. Course, in my opinion, Badger's brainpan wouldn't hold enough water to satisfy a meat wasp."

"He ain't too smart, but he's tough as whang leather. You got to improvise," Givens said. "Hell, man, when I was riding for Stonewall, nothing ever went as planned. Improvise was the word of the day, every day."

"Well, General Stonewall," Blodget said, "get to doin' it."

"Let's just let them old boys ride on by. They's five of them, which means they done left only one man at the ranch with the McKeag woman. We'll just go on down to the ranch house and take care of that part of the problem. Strike where they's weakest, that's what ol' Stonewall would do."

Blodget merely shrugged.

"Besides," Al continued, "the woman is there, and I hear she shines like a new penny." He patted his sideburns down as he spoke, as if grooming would help.

"We got a job to do, Givens. You worry about that old boy down there, and about the money that's waiting should we finish this."

"Go to hell, Blodget. I'll worry about what I want to worry about. You just pull your weight."

"Keep quiet. Those riders is already halfway here."

They reined deeper into the copse of trees, two hundred yards above the creek trail they'd crossed, quieted the horses as best they could, and waited.

★ ★ ★

Tom Macklin set the pace on his dun mule, with young Roan just behind riding a rank little mustang that he'd caught and broke himself. The little paint horse was all heart, and with Tom's help, Roan had turned him into a fine animal, if one that still had too much gumption for his own good.

Slim John rode behind Roan, and Poker Pete behind him. Skeeter McKelvie brought up the rear.

They'd just started up the canyon where the trail began a series of switchbacks when Tom reined the dun mule up and sat staring at the ground.

"What?" Roan asked.

Tom turned back to the others. "Any of you fellas up here yesterday?" All of them shook their heads. "Well, we had a couple of riders pass by here, maybe even today by the looks of this track. Could be Bar X boys snoopin' around, or could just be somebody passin' through."

"Shoulda stopped at the place, if they was passin' on by," Roan said.

"Shoulda," Tom agreed, "but some folks is just not sociable." Tom waved Skeeter on up. "You want the west side of the canyon?"

"Good as any," Skeeter said.

"Then you take Pete and break off here. Work your way around the west side of the mountaintop and follow Cedar Creek a ways, then cut up and over the ridge into Deep Creek. We'll work the east side."

Skeeter nodded, but before he reined away, Tom cautioned him. "I don't take to folks riding around the home place. Seems like mischief to me. Keep a sharp eye. Wouldn't hurt nothing if you followed that track a ways before you cut off."

Skeeter nodded, waved to Poker Pete to follow, and set off across the little creek. Tom, Roan, and Slim John continued up the switchback, away from Spotted Dog Creek.

The Bar X hands had been harassing Lucky Seven riders for the last couple of years, and had even tried to build a ditch higher up the mountain to divert Spotted Dog Creek away from the Lucky Seven at a spot where it crossed government land belonging to neither ranch. Prager had long coveted the water from Spotted Dog. Dan McKeag had put an end to that effort when he faced down Dirk Prager, only to have young Prager draw on him and try to back-shoot Dan. From only twenty feet, Prager's shot went wild. Dan's first one didn't, square in the center of Prager's breastbone. He didn't live two heartbeats. Dan later said that the whine of a bullet is hint enough in any man's language, and needs answering.

From that time on, Lucky Seven hands had to live with the occasional wild shot their way when they neared the common border of the two ranches.

There were over twenty Bar X hands, some of them, Dan had suspected, hired not for their cowhand abilities, but for their gun skills.

Dan knew it was about to come to a head when he'd set out for Helena, and was not surprised when he'd been warned by an old friend in Helena, the desk man at the Palace Hotel, that the rumor about town was that Prager had some hired men waiting for his arrival.

Badger and Slater rode hard, pushing their horses up a long slope of thick fir until they reached a wide trail used by the cattle, as well as elk and deer, to move up and down from Spotted Dog Creek to the high meadows on the slopes of McKeag's Mountain. Badger figured the Lucky Seven riders were on their way up the mountain to check the calf crop, and maybe even to brand what they found. He still had no idea how to handle the situation if there were five of them, but he'd cross that bridge when he came to it.

Men and horses were well winded by the time they got into position on a rock outcropping where they could watch a spot fifty yards below where the trail opened onto the first of a series of wide meadows that fell away down the mountainside. It was mid-morning by the time three riders came into sight.

"Only three," Badger said to Slater in a low voice.

"Let's take 'em," Slater said. All of the Bar X hirelings were well armed with Winchesters provided by Prager.

"Maybe they'll split up later?" Badger said.

"And maybe they won't," Slater said in a low voice as he rose. He closed his bad eye, and leveled the rifle at the first rider.

"That's the young'un in the lead. Take the second, when they come even with us, and I'll take the last. We can run down the kid later should he bolt."

Roan was in the lead, with Slim John following. Tom Macklin was riding drag.

Slater centered the sights on the man in the middle, and Al Givens on the black man riding the mule.

It was Slater who pulled off first, blowing Slim John from the saddle. Givens fired quickly, but the mule had shied back, almost throwing Tom from the saddle.

Tom dropped, taking his shotgun with him, rolling under the low limbs of a chokecherry.

"Ride," Tom yelled at Roan. The boy gave heels to the little mustang, and the game horse was across the meadow and into the trees in three leaps.

Roan reined up quickly when he reached cover and spun the animal back, but could see Tom waving madly at him, shooing him, like he would a pest, telling him to ride on. Roan glanced up the hill to see two riders, each carrying a long arm, mounting fast-looking horses.

Even though he terribly wanted to ride back to check on Tom and Slim John, he did as told and quirted the mustang until he was moving at a full gallop across the side hill.

He hadn't covered more than fifty yards when he looked over his shoulder to see the two riders coming hard behind him. Without hesitating, Roan jerked rein right, down the steep mountainside, crashing into thick boughs of fir. The limbs clawed at him, trying to jerk him out of the saddle, but he clung, hunkering low so the horse's head and neck took the worst of it.

The mustang found a game trail, and broke right again, back the way they'd come. It opened some, and he was again running hard.

They broke back out into the meadow and Roan reined the mustang back up the hill, back to the spot where they'd been ambushed.

He jerked rein when he saw Tom under the chokecherry.

"Are they behind you?" Tom yelled at him.

"Close," Roan yelled.

"Keep riding, I'll lay for them."

"You're hit," Roan said, starting to dismount when he saw the plume of blood low on Tom's shirt.

"No, Roan. Ride, all the way back to the ranch. John's dead. Get help!"

"They'll shoot you down, Tom," Roan said, fear echoing in his voice.

"Ride, boy, ride. It's our only chance."

Tom chucked a rock at the mustang's flank, and the horse shot forward, just as two riders broke out of the fir forest behind them.

Tom sank deeper into the chokecherry,

deep enough where he hoped he was un-seen.

In moments the riders were even with him, then pounded on by in pursuit of the boy.

Tom rolled out of the low branches, came up on one knee, hoped his barrels weren't full of meadow trash, and fired one barrel of the double at the nearest rider's back. The man was thirty yards or more down the trail by the time Tom got a bead on him, but the shot knocked him forward in the saddle. To Tom's dismay, he kept riding.

"Damn. Come on back, you slimy bastards!" Tom yelled after them, but they rode on disappearing into the trees.

Tom tried to rise, but the pain in his side drove him back to one knee. He tried again, desperate to get to his mule to follow and protect the boy, but he couldn't seem to find the strength.

He used the shotgun as a crutch, and got to his feet, struggling toward his mule, who had run some distance away but was grazing back toward him. It was the third mule he'd had since he'd come to Montana, and would come to a whistle, as all of them would. But Tom couldn't seem to get enough wind to whistle.

The mule looked up from grazing, but then began to tumble, at least in Tom's vision. The whole world was tumbling. Tom went to his knees, then to his back, his eyes tightly closed, his breath coming in short gasps. Things faded and all went quiet.

Roan, pounding hard, reached another opening, this one a one-hundred-pace-long escarpment of shale, falling away steeply to his left. He took a deep breath and jerked rein, aiming the little mustang straight down the rock. The horse alternated between running, then setting his forelegs when he got going too fast, starting small rock slides, but he kept his feet under him even though Roan thought they'd go head over heels.

Roan reined up where the slope leveled off into a thick copse of lodgepole pine, and looked back up the steep slope.

Badger reined up when he realized where the boy had taken the little horse. He scratched his head in wonder.

"Damn," he said, staring after him, "little som'bitch got more sand than the Mojave." Badger was a brave and tough man, but not brave nor confident enough with his animal to charge down what was practically a cliff.

He turned when he heard the clicking hoofs of another horse behind him, and was surprised to see Slater lying across his saddle horn, his face alongside the horse's neck.

"You shot?" he asked the tall man.

"Shot all to hell," Slater said. "My whole back's on fire."

Badger let him come even, and then saw the dozen small holes in the back of Slater's frock coat. "Damned if you didn't take a load of buckshot to the back. You gonna die on me?"

"How the hell do I know," Slater said, anger ringing in his voice. "I ain't no prophet."

Badger sighed deeply. "You won't be worth a bent horseshoe nail to me if'n you're dead. We'll worry on the boy later. Let's find a spot to dismount, and I'll see how bad you're shot up . . . and if I can dig any of that scattergun lead outta your ugly hide."

Chapter 7

Erin McKeag helped Simon with the breakfast cleanup, then retired to her cabin to catch up on her sewing. Simon went to the barn to repair a broken singletree and work on worn and broken tack.

She was continually distracted by thoughts of Dan, worrying about why he hadn't shown up as of yet. It was mid-morning, with her in the middle of sewing in a new panel on the quilt she'd been working on for months, when she heard the clomp-clomp of hoofbeats. She ran to the ranch house door, ready to run into Dan's arms. Her face fell when she saw a pair of strangers, both in ankle-length dusters, dismounting at the hitching rail across the yard at the barn. The day was already warming, and she thought the dusters strange.

Simon's big frame filled the door to the tack room, a leather apron adorning his wide girth, tongs in one hand and hammer in the other. Erin didn't know why, but she felt a shudder down her backbone and shut the door, then reached over it and fetched down the double-barrel shotgun Dan kept there.

Maybe it was the fact Simon didn't have a smile on his face, maybe it was the fact both men pulled long arms from their saddle scabbards as they dismounted. Both were strangers to Erin, and it was not like her not to welcome strangers with a cup of coffee if it was cold or a glass of cold water if warm. But the look of these two belied that.

Simon Coppersmith was already a little wary, as he'd thought he'd heard the report of more than one shot far up the mountain, but it was so distant he couldn't be sure. He eyed the two carefully as they dismounted, and when he saw them pulling rifles from scabbards, he dropped the tongs, reached beside the door, and rested his hand on the Springfield .45-70 that leaned against the frame.

"Good morning," the taller of the two said with a crooked smile.

"Morning," Simon echoed, studying the man.

"We're passing through, thought you might share a bit of water for the animals, and maybe for us?"

"You Bar X hands?"

"What's the Bar X?" the smaller of the two said, shrugging a little too convincingly. "We're over from Bozeman way."

"Yer travelin' light for being this far from nowhere, and a long way from the Mullan Trail."

It was the taller who spoke up. "Riding town to town, checking the country out, on our way to Oregon if we don't come on something suits us better."

Simon had yet to smile, and this information didn't comfort him. "You can see the well 'twixt here and the house. Help yourself . . . then be on your way." The two stood ten feet away, smiling in a distracting manner, not making a move to the well. Simon's tone lowered a little when he asked, "You need those Winchesters to water stock — or yourself for that matter?"

The men started to spread apart, a move that was as threatening to Simon as if they'd raised the rifles, so he snatched the Springfield away from the door frame, raising it and cocking it in one motion . . . but he wasn't fast enough.

The taller man's rifle roared, knocking Simon back into the tack room and over a draw-down table, knocking it one way and the saddle that rested on it the other.

Saddle-maker's tools scattered over the packed dirt floor.

But Simon was a hard man who'd taken a bullet before in the war, and was not out of it. The shorter man filled the doorway, and Simon managed to fire the Springfield. The man spun out of the doorway, out of Simon's view. The shot had taken Simon high in the left shoulder, and he scrambled to break the trapdoor breech of the Springfield to reload, while at the same time pulling a fresh shell from a leather bandolier encircling the rifle's butt, but his left arm wouldn't work.

The other man stepped into the door, blocking the light, levering in another shell. Then seeing Simon's predicament, he slowed and stepped inside, just out of Simon's kicking range.

"You scum-suckin' swine bastard," Simon managed before the man leveled the Winchester. The man smiled, and the lever action roared again. This shot took Simon in the middle of the breastbone, and his big frame rolled to the side with a shudder. By the third stuttering heartbeat, all went black.

"Unlike yer'sef, I know my ma and pa, and they was married in a proper church," Blodget said with a snarl as he stepped forward and poked the big man in his thick thigh with the barrel of the Winchester.

He turned to see Al Givens on the ground, whining as if he'd had a leg blown off. Blodget walked over and bent over Givens. "You damn fool, the shot cut a groove in your belt. You ain't even bleedin'. Get up off your duff and hunt up somethin' to use for a backbone."

Givens, patting his belly and side searching for a wound, got a relieved if stupid look on his face, then climbed to his feet, just as a shutter on the ranch house, forty paces across the yard, swung aside, and a double-barreled shotgun barrel poked through.

"Blodget!" Givens managed to yell as he dove to the side, but the shotgun let loose both barrels before either of them could move far.

Buckshot splattered Blodget, spinning him around and knocking him down; then the shutter slammed shut again.

"Damn that whore," Blodget managed, struggling to his feet. But the heavy canvas duster had taken the most of the dissipated shot, and only a few had found their way to flesh. He stumbled inside the tack room, quickly followed by Givens.

"That was the woman?" Givens asked.

"It was," he said, carefully peeling the coat away. "You said she was a looker. She don't look so handsome staring down the barrel of that scattergun." Blodget wiped the back of his head and neck, coming away with a palm smeared with blood. "I'm going to split her gullet," Blodget snarled.

Givens smiled. "Before or after I dig them pellets outta your back?"

"After. I got a bottle of Who Hit John in my saddlebags. Fetch it out afore we start."

While Badger Hotchkins sat high on the hill working on Slater's back, Givens sat in the McKeag storeroom, doing the same to Blodget. Badger and Slater had done far more damage than they'd received, but Badger was beginning to wonder.

"Where the hell is Givens and Blodget?" he asked, more of himself than Slater.

"Dunno. Dang it, Badger, be careful. That ain't no saddle you're working on."

"You're lucky it ain't, or I'd just throw it in the scrap pile. I thought we finished that black beggar, but I guess he's still shakin' or I wouldn't be having to pick you like a goose."

"Can you get 'em all?"

"Doubt it. Some is deeper'un you want me diggin'."

"Do your best. I want to get back up there and repay the favor."

It took Badger more than an hour to get all the buckshot out that he could feel under the skin, having to leave a half-dozen pellets where they were.

He cleaned his knife blade on his pant leg, then snapped, "Get yer shirt on so's we can get down the hill after that boy."

"Bull. I want to go back and kill that black bastard."

"He ain't going nowhere. He was hit right and good, blood everywhere. We got to get the boy, afore he gets down the mountain to warn the ranch."

"How 'bout the other two?"

"They was all carryin' lariats and bedrolls . . . wouldn't a had bedrolls if they was just out for the day . . . and one of 'em had a pack behind the saddle that looked like it might carry grub for a couple of days. I think they were headed up the mountain on a chore that will last overnight. Let's get the boy, then go after the others . . . we can track down the black when we come back. He was hit hard, and is probably bled out already."

"Okay, the boy, but then the black."

They mounted up and started back down the mountain, carefully picking their way down the rocky escarpment until they picked up Roan's trail.

"He's moving hard and fast," Slater observed, closing his bad eye and noting the length of the little paint horse's strides.

"Then we got to move faster," Badger said, gigging his horse into a lope.

Tennessee Tom Macklin awoke, his side soaked in blood, blood soaked into the soil where he lay. He wondered how much blood he'd lost, but knew he hadn't lost as much as Slim John, who lay a dozen paces away, his head cocked at a funny angle, his legs and arms askew. It was obvious he hadn't moved since he was blown from his horse. The paint he rode grazed a few steps down the slope, the mule a few steps farther on.

Tom managed to sit up, and to whistle at the dun mule. The animal's ears tilted forward, and he stood for a moment as if irritated at being called away from the sweet grass underfoot, but training overcame, and soon he was moving up toward Tom, dragging his reins.

"Don't step on them reins," Tom managed, as if the mule understood. He gasped for a moment, his side sore as a cut carbuncle.

But the mule avoided the trailing reins and came close enough that Tom could gather them in hand. He managed to pull himself to a standing position, the solid old mule standing while he did so. Tom turned the stirrup forward, trying to mount as he normally did, but couldn't raise his boot high enough to settle it in the inviting opening. He had to get mounted, or he knew he'd die here on this mountainside.

He limped over to a rock outcropping, leading the mule, positioned the animal, and inched and winced his way up on an eighteen-inch rock. Managing to throw a leg over the mule, he struggled into the saddle.

He knew a place, if he could only get there, and it wasn't more than a mile, maybe less. It would keep him out of the weather, and maybe keep them from finding him, should they come back to finish the job — whoever *they* were.

Through the crack between the shutters, Erin had seen Simon blown back into his tack room. She'd been unable to control herself, and had thrown open the shutters to get a shot off at the intruders, knocking one of them from his feet.

But it now appeared her rash action

would cost her. The men, including the one she hoped she'd sent to his maker, were circling the house in different directions, looking, she feared, for a way to get to her.

Fetching the box of shotgun shells from Dan's gun cabinet, she reloaded the spent barrel, then took a position in the rocking chair, facing the door, and rocked and patiently waited.

Blodget worked his way around the south side of the house, keeping the corral and a small grouping of fruit trees between himself and the windows. The woman appeared to be adept with the shotgun, and his back would already take weeks to mend. He had no desire for a face full of buckshot, or having his head blown off.

Givens had gone to the north side of the east-facing house. Blodget knew that Givens had a taste for the woman — he'd apparently seen her somewhere before — and decided he'd bide his time. Givens was prodded by something more than just doing the job and collecting their pay. Blodget knew if he waited, Givens would press the house. They had time, so long as the Lucky Seven hands didn't reappear.

Blodget positioned himself behind a

corral post, his attention on the window on his side of the house, dug the makings out of his shirt pocket, rolled and lit a cigarette, and waited.

Roan McKeag had heard the gunshots from the direction of the ranch buildings as he approached, and cautiously reined the mustang up the mountain behind the house.

He dismounted, leaving the horse tied in a copse of lodgepole, and made his way to a rock outcropping a hundred yards above the ranch house. A woodpile adorned the back of the house, as well as a door to the root cellar, a back door leading into the kitchen, and a single window Roan knew was at the house's one bedroom.

Between the toe of the slope and the back door was the privy.

Two horses were tied at the hitching rail outside the tack room. He saw a man moving around to the north side of the house, then with careful study, another in the horse corral on the south. The way the first man moved and the second hid made it clear they were up to no good.

What was happening? They were attacked on the trail by strange riders, and now strangers were stalking the ranch house.

Where was Simon? Inside with Erin? Or had they already shot him down? Simon was a hard man; he'd related many wartime and Indian-fighting episodes to Roan, and Roan couldn't imagine him shot down.

But he was nowhere in sight.

Roan decided he had to get in the house. But how?

He carried a LeMat revolver, a gift from Dan, who'd taken the weapon off a Confederate colonel during the war. It was a lot of gun for a fourteen-year-old, heavy and a little cumbersome with a six-and-a-half-inch rifled barrel in .44 caliber, over a unique smooth-bore 20-gauge single-shot shotgun barrel. He carried no extra shells, but had five in the revolver and a 20-gauge brass in the shotgun barrel. Dan had given him the revolver so he could shoot the occasional grouse he came across.

With the two men so close to the house, Roan decided to circle around and approach the barn and tack room from the rear. He studied the country, and thought he could reach Spotted Dog Creek without being seen. The creek cut into the valley floor, and Roan knew he could follow it to a point only a hundred yards from the barn, then ride like hell up and out of the rift to the rear of the barn and inside if need be. If he could do that without being seen, it was only forty more yards to the house, and the stone enclosure of the well offered cover halfway between.

The man on the north side of the house had made his way to the structure, and was flattened against it, long arm at his side, inching along to the window, when Roan scrambled back up the hill to the mustang and mounted up. In a few minutes he was three hundred yards up the valley, out of the brush, and into the rift of the creek. In a few more, he was dismounted again, lying on the creek bed's edge, again studying the situation.

The man who'd been on the north side must be at the rear, out of Roan's sight. The other man still stood at the corral fence post, smoking, watching the house, his long arm casually in the crook of his elbow.

Roan mounted back up, and since the man on the north side was out of sight, decided a stealthy approach was best. He carefully kept the barn between himself and the man on the south at the corral, and let the mustang walk itself to the rear of the barn — where he was more than willing to go, as the barn meant grain to the horses.

Roan dismounted, tied the mustang to a fence rail at the rear of the barn, and carefully entered. He let his eyes adjust to the darkness, making sure the other man had not snuck back to the barn. But there was no one. The barn was empty except for the two draft horses Dan used for the plow, the freight wagon, and other heavy work.

One of them nickered quietly at Roan as he tiptoed across the straw-covered floor to the barn entry into the tack room.

Roan quietly opened the door, studied the interior, then slipped in when satisfied it was empty. Then he stopped short, taking a deep gasp when he saw his old friend Simon on the floor, his chest covered with drying blood, his eyes open and staring.

Chapter 8

Roan's chest tightened, emotions flooding him: anger, anguish, fear. He collected himself, knowing that he had to get to Erin before she too lay blood-soaked, eyes staring blankly.

What would Dan do?

Roan, breathing heavily from the shock of seeing Simon, moved to the outside door, quietly opened it a couple of inches, and looked to find the intruders . . . the murderers.

The man at the corral was still there, the other still out of sight.

The men's two horses were tied only steps from the door. Roan slipped out to set them free, then saw the shining Sharps rifle on one of the saddles, and a leather case hanging from the saddle horn. The box had a row of shell pockets, each with a .45-90 shell protruding. He moved out, slipped the long rifle out and the case off the saddle horn, then returned to the tack room. The rifle was new, without a scratch, and the box contained loading gear: a bullet mold, powder, spare cartridge cases, and lead.

He checked the chamber and found the Sharps loaded, pulled out four more shells and fitted them between his fingers, then again moved outside. He slipped the bridles off the horses, leaving their reins tied to the hitching post, but setting them free. Carefully keeping the well between him and the man at the corral, hunkering low, he quickly closed the twenty yards to where he could hide with the stone walls of the well as protection.

Then he saw the other man, on the roof of the house, messing about the stovepipe. Erin had built an early morning fire to ward off the chill, and a wisp of smoke still sent tendrils skyward. As Roan watched, the man pulled his duster off and fitted it over the stovepipe.

Roan was positive he couldn't make it the rest of the way to the house without being seen, so he selected the only alternative.

He broke and ran, yelling as he did. "Aunt Erin! Let me in! Open the door!"

By the time he reached the door, Erin was removing the bar. Before the man at the corral could reposition himself to get a shot off, and before the man on the roof could make it to the roof's edge, Roan was inside.

"They killed Simon," both of them said at once.

"And Slim John," Roan added. "There's more of them up the mountain. Tom's shot bad. We got to get rid of these two, and get back up there."

"Hold on, Roan, calm down," Erin said.

"We got to get back up there. . . ."

"First we've got to stay alive. Tom will have to wait."

"What should we do?"

"Wait. Dan will be back, or the others . . . where's Skeeter and Pete?"

"We split up earlier. They were to go down the west side of the gorge and we were gonna take the east."

"Maybe they heard the shots?" Erin suggested.

"Maybe. Let's get that fire out," Roan said, noticing that the stove was beginning to leak smoke. Then he explained, "The one on the roof blocked the stovepipe."

Erin quickly opened the fire door and dumped the last of her morning's coffee onto the coals. It steamed and fizzled out quickly.

"What's going on, Aunt Erin?" Roan asked.

"It's the Bar X . . . Prager. He wants this place and Dan won't sell. I know this has to be Prager's doing."

They heard a man curse as it seemed he'd jumped from the roof to the top of the woodpile, and they heard wood tumble and him crash to the ground.

"Hope he broke his damned neck," Erin said, uncharacteristically cursing, giving Roan a reassuring wink.

"Now what?"

"We wait. They'll get hungry or tired and leave."

"I hope. Tom is lying up there."

"Tom's tough. We can't do him any good if we can't get up there . . . ever."

Young Roan sighed deeply.

Givens slipped away from the back of the house and ran for the corral, sliding under the bottom rail, catching his breath, then pulling himself up to stand beside Blodget.

"That was the boy what got in the house?"

"It was. Little whelp done stole my Sharps too."

"The hell you say." Givens face fell. "Damn . . . and the horses done wandered off!"

"He must have turned 'em out. He's

getting to be a real pain where Dr. Stolderhachim's pill won't get to."

"What?"

"A pain in the ass, Givens. You're a mite slow."

"It ain't *my* rifle the boy's got," Givens snarled, turning red in the face. "It weren't me let him sneak up on the horses and turn 'em loose. Seems as you may be slow as a slug, Blodget."

Blodget eyed Givens, thinking how much he'd enjoy cracking him on the head with his Winchester, but didn't. He wanted this to end, and fighting with Givens didn't seem the way to make it happen. He turned his attention to the house for a moment, then said in a low voice, "Let's burn them out."

Givens stared at him for a minute, then said, "That woman won't be worth a damn if'n she's done to a turn."

Blodget sighed deeply, then snapped, "To hell with you lusting after the woman. Let's make this end."

"You'll burn yer Sharps up."

That did take Blodget back a moment; then he shrugged his shoulders. "I'll have plenty of money to buy another. 'Sides, the boy will bring it out with him when he makes a break."

"Sure hate to burn that woman," Givens said, a woeful look on his face.

"There's a flock of women in Seattle. I thought you said you wanted to go there."

"I do. I am. But there ain't many women like that one anywheres."

"The rest of the Lucky Seven riders might come along any time, if Badger and Slater didn't do their job." Blodget hitched up his pants and slipped though the fence, then turned back to Givens. "Try and watch the front of the house," Blodget said, then broke for the back at a run, his Winchester in one hand, his Colt in the other.

In moments, Givens saw a wisp of smoke rise from the back of the house. He moved so he had a clear view of the front door, positioned his Winchester on a top rail of the corral fence, and waited.

Blodget got the woodpile burning, then moved up the hill away from the house where he'd have a clear view of the rear door. He too found a rest for his rifle against a lodgepole pine. He knew it wouldn't be long.

Erin had peeked through the crack between the shutters on the rear windows, and seen Blodget's back as he hurried up the hill. She opened the shutters just far enough to see the mischief he'd been up to.

"My God," she managed.

"What?" Roan asked.

"They've set the woodpile afire. We don't have long. . . ."

Roan scratched his head, then suggested, "Let's make them think we're coming out the front, then make a run for it out the back?"

"Or just give up and see what they want?"

"Did they give Simon a chance to give up?"

Erin sighed deeply. "No. They shot him down like a dog."

"Then that settles it."

"How do we make them think we're going out the front?"

"Open the door and chuck some things out."

Smoke was beginning to seep between the joints of the logs at the rear of the house, the chinking itself beginning to smolder.

A ladder-back rocker was one of the few things Erin had brought to the ranch, one of the few things she'd considered her own. "Throw out the rocker," she instructed, hoping to save it if possible.

Roan set aside the Sharps, which he'd

kept in hand since crashing into the house, and picked up the rocker. Erin swung the door aside, and he flung it out. Then he grabbed up a stool. He flung out three more items before they ran to the rear. Erin peeked out between the shutters, looking for the man who'd gone upslope, but could see him nowhere in the trees.

Erin coughed and hacked, the smoke beginning to choke her. "Better go," she said to Roan, who slammed open the rear door, and they burst through.

Erin carried the double-barrel shotgun, and Roan the Sharps as well as the kit with bullet mold and lead. He also had the LeMat on his hip.

But he kept it holstered so he could help Erin. He took her left hand in his right. Each of them had a long arm in the other.

It was less than thirty yards to the edge of the lodgepoles, but uphill.

They ran for all they were worth, but just before reaching the trees, a man stepped out of the trees twenty paces away, raising his rifle.

Roan shoved Erin on toward the tree line, dropping to one knee and cocking the Sharps in the same motion, but the man's Winchester went off before he could get the weapon in place. Erin stumbled and went to the ground before she reached the tree line.

The Sharps spun out of Roan's grasp, its stock shattered.

The man swung his weapon on Erin as she was on her knees raising the shotgun. He fired again, and she was blown backward onto her back on the hillside.

"Erin!" Roan yelled, grabbing at the LeMat and wrestling it from its holster on his hip. He cocked the 20-gauge barrel and fired as the man was levering in another shell. One of the man's legs went out from under him and he tumbled back into the tree line, screaming as he did so.

Roan turned to his aunt, who was grasping her chest with both hands, her face a mask of anguish.

He reholstered the LeMat as plumes of dirt rose around him, and he realized the other man was shooting at him from the corral, seventy-five yards away.

Scrambling up the hill, he grasped Erin's wrist and began to drag her up the hill to the cover of the trees. Two more shots were fired at them before he managed to get her under the low, thick branches of some underbrush.

He dropped to his knees and tried to

stem the bleeding from Erin's chest, but he could see it was futile.

"Wait," she managed to whisper, a thin line of blood already trickling from the side of her mouth. She reached up with a tender hand and cupped his cheek.

He stopped, tears flooding his eyes.

"Tell Dan I love him. Now go."

"I can't," Roan said.

"Please . . . go . . . Roan. Take care of . . ." Her breath rattled once, then again, then stopped.

Roan screamed. "No! No!" Then another shot struck the ground near his hiding place. He reached over and tenderly closed Erin's eyes, took a deep breath, gathered himself to run, then realized he'd left the Sharps back on the hillside. Quick as a cat he was out of the brush and had it, then crashed into the trees and on up the hill.

He didn't stop running until he'd circled the place, found his way back to the creek bed, and went up it to the back of the barn. He was on the mustang and pounding across the valley, with his chest heaving and the wind blowing his tears away.

He didn't rein up until he'd crossed the valley and reached the line of firs on the foot of McKeag's Mountain.

Only then, taking deep gasping breaths, did he shake his fist at the men below.

"I'll kill you all," he shouted. "All of you. Every damned one of you." His throat closed and his eyes flooded again. He turned the little mustang up the hill, gigging him into a hard climb. He looked back only one more time, to see the ranch house totally involved in flames, and muttered, "As God is my witness, I'll kill every damn one of them." Who exactly he didn't know, but he knew the killing had just begun. Erin said it was Prager and the Bar X, and that was good enough for Roan.

He knew a place where he could hide, where they'd never find him. He'd go there, and get ready.

Chapter 9

Dan McKeag awoke with a start.

No one was in the room.

"Pad!" He called out. Getting no answer, he tried to remember the woman's name, but couldn't. "Hey, anyone."

No one answered. Something was nagging at him terribly. He knew by the way his chest felt, a deep throbbing ache, that he should stay right where he was, but he couldn't, he had to get up, he had to get back to the Lucky Seven.

With great effort he kicked the covers away. The tops of his long handles had been sliced away, bandages in their place, but the bottoms were intact. He dropped one leg to the floor, and cried out in pain as he did so, but he managed to sit up. Gasping, he sat for a moment, his head hanging. With supreme effort, he dropped the other leg to the floor, pivoting to sit on the edge of the bed.

God, he was weak. He tried to heave himself to his feet, but kept going, pitched forward, and fell hard on his face.

He didn't know how long he lay there, but he awoke with Pad trying to get him to his feet.

"Pad . . . where's Erin?"

Pad dragged him up, with Blue at his side, whining like a puppy. "Let me get you back to bed, you damn fool. Where'd you think you was going?"

"Where's Erin?"

"Haven't heard from her yet. I sent another telegram."

With care, Pad managed to get him seated on the edge of the bed, then swung his legs up and covered him with the patchwork quilt.

"You need the chamber pot?"

"Later. Where's Erin?"

"Dan, I haven't heard from her. I went out to take Blue to do his business. Hell's bells, man, you got to stay in bed till you mend."

"How long's it been?"

"You been in bed most a week."

"So I've . . . been gone from the ranch . . . what . . . ten days?"

"Eleven or twelve, I think."

"Then something's . . . wrong. Bad wrong. Pad, you've got to go to the Lucky Seven . . . and check . . . on Erin and Roan."

108

"Lay quiet and catch yer breath, Dan."

"You've got to go."

"Go where?" Rose Ballard was in the doorway.

"He wants me to go over the mountain to the Lucky Seven," Pad said, his tone a little exasperated.

Rose walked over and patted Dan's hand. "You're worried."

"I should have heard from my wife."

"Then go, Padraig. I can take care of things here."

"Not with this damn fool trying to get out and take a hike," Pad said, his hands on hips.

"Toby has the gout and is not worth a damn downstairs. I've got to get another swamper to fill in for him. Now that Mr. McKeag is eating and seems to want to wander about, I'm moving him out into the sitting room where old Toby can stay with him. . . . That way I can have my room back."

Dan flushed, then his face colored. "I don't mean . . . to seem . . . unappreciative, ma'am."

"Rose. Please, Dan, you've been in my bed for days. You can call me Rose."

"Rose. Pad, you get me a wagon, make a bed in the back, and take me to the ranch."

"Ha," Pad said. "You ain't going nowhere for at least a week. Doc says —"

"The hell with the doc. I've got to get —"

"Well," Pad said adamantly, "is what you've got to get. I'll go to the Lucky Seven and fetch Erin if that'll shut you up. But you've got to promise to stay where you are for at least a week."

Dan hesitated for a long moment, realizing that he couldn't even stand, much less ride. He relented. "I'll stay . . . for a few more days. Five days it'll take . . . two to get there, stay a day . . . and two to get back. Take Dancer, and don't . . . tarry. I'm worried sick."

"You're dog-sick, is what you are."

"I'll watch him," Rose said, smiling, again patting Dan on the hand.

"Ride hard, Pad," Dan said.

Pad nodded, and left. He had to head over to his little room at Miss Maddy's Boarding House and fix up a bedroll.

As he pushed through the bat-wing doors of the Bonny Glen, he ran flush into the fat Helena deputy Howard Perkins.

"Slow down there, Paddy."

"Mornin', Perkins," Pad said, trying to skirt the man, but the deputy grabbed him by the arm.

"Where you been, Paddy? I ain't seen

you since your bother-in-law was planted."

"I been busy."

"Heard you got the boot at the bank."

Pad had never liked Perkins, and the hair came up on the back of his neck with the deputy's tone. "I quit, if'n it's any of your affair, Perkins."

"So, I hear you've been spendin' your time upstairs in the Bonny?"

Pad stepped close to Perkins, almost face-to-face with the man. Paddy, the shorter of the two, had to gaze up. "You worry about what goes on down here on the streets, Perkins. You stay out of folks' personal business."

Perkins guffawed, backing away a step. "So it's true. You been keepin' company with Miss Rose?"

Paddy stayed after him, and shoved Perkins against the front wall of the Bonny Glen, then put a finger in the big man's face. "Miss Ballard is a fine lady, and I'll be pleased . . . no, right anxious . . . to bust out the teeth of the man who says otherwise."

Perkins's face flushed; then he tried to recover his composure by snarling, "I'm a lawman, Dundee. You could end up coolin' yer heels in the rat cage this town calls a jail."

Now Pad shoved his stubby finger deep into the soft spot just below Perkins's sternum. "And you could end up being the party with a fine place to suck his cigar . . . where his teeth used to be. More'n one man has found that whippin' me is tough as scratchin' yer ear with your elbow, but if you'd like to try —"

"Cool down, Paddy. I didn't mean nothin'."

"Then don't say nothin'." Pad settled down, taking a deep breath. "I got business." He spun on his heel and limped away toward Miss Maddy's.

Perkins stood looking at the bat-wing doors of the Bonny Glen, wondering if it was true that Paddy had been keeping close company with Rose Ballard. He couldn't imagine the man being that lucky, but stranger things had happened in Helena.

It took Roan two hours to ride up to the cave, which was between the ranch buildings and where he'd left Tom. He wanted to check on the cave to make sure it was a good place to bring Tom, if he was still alive. He and Tennessee Tom had found the cave the year before, and marveled at the paintings, scratchins Roan called them,

112

on its wall. Stick drawings of animals and hunters covered almost twenty feet in length of the outside chamber, as high as a man could reach. They hadn't been discovered until he and Tom had made torches with the intent of exploring deeper than the first chamber. The chamber was dark, as only a tall two-foot-wide rift in the ancient sediment rock exposed it. It was a strange place in the mountain, where sediment rock came up next to solid. Tom had explained to him what sediment rock was, and shown him how it was made up of something like a streambed, or ocean bottom, that had once covered this whole area. Then in places, it looked as if a giant hand had turned the world on end. The layers were angled steeply. It was in the intersection of one of these steeply angled layers and the solid rock where the cave had formed, and the paintings were on the solid rock face.

It was a good place to camp. And had been for a time longer than Roan liked to think about. Fire rings were everywhere on the five-by-twenty-five-pace floor in the outer chamber.

It would be a good place to hide out, a good place from which to hunt. He could even bring the little mustang inside. The

113

rock face leading up to the cave would keep others from following track there, and a pair of high elderberry bushes shielded the entrance so you had to be looking to know it was there. It was a lush crop of elderberries that had led him and Tom to discover the place in the first instance — elderberries that Erin had made delicious jam out of while Tom and Roan had told her of their find.

Erin would make no more jam, Roan thought as he crossed the rock face to the cave entrance, but then again, a lot of Bar X hands would not live to see another elderberry-picking season.

Roan tied the mustang to a lodgepole pine growing from a fissure in the rock, then jumped back, slapping for the LeMat on his hip, as a horse whinnied almost on top of them. The mustang answered.

He palmed the big revolver and searched in all directions for the animal, and its possible rider, but no one was to be seen. Then a low nicker came from nearby . . . and Roan realized the sounds were coming out of the cave.

Slowly, he moved to the bushes. He shut his eyes for a moment, so they'd be adjusted to the darkness, then opened them as he charged in, quickly diving to the side so his silhouette wouldn't be framed in the opening.

"Who's there?" he said.

Nearby, the nicker came again. Roan's eyes weren't quite there yet, but he could clearly hear slow hoof falls as an animal moved closer, then stepped into the light.

It wasn't a horse at all. It was Grunt, Tom's old mule.

"Tom!" Roan called out. Tom had made it to the cave — he must be all right.

A groan came from deeper in the cave.

Roan moved quickly forward, almost stumbling over Tom, who lay on his back stretched below the wall of drawings.

Roan kneeled next to his friend. "Tom. You're still bleeding." Blood had continued to seep from the wound in Tom's side. Maybe too much blood, as he seemed to be unconscious, near death. He did not respond.

Now what to do? Roan thought. *I'll collect some wood and build a fire and make sure it's warm enough for Tom tonight. If he lives until night.*

But first, a bed. Roan fetched the mustang and led him inside, then stripped away both the saddles. Luckily, Tom had been carrying the rucksack full of grub for the five of them. Roan made a bed from

115

the saddle blankets and Tom's bedroll, then led the animals outside. He moved away from the cave to the nearest meadow, almost a quarter mile from the cave. A trickle of water cut a slight indentation in the meadow, so Roan searched until he found a place to set up a picket line that crossed the tiny stream. The banks were lush with grass, and using the animals' lead ropes, he tied them to the picket line so they could feed and water. Satisfied that they'd be fine for at least a full day, he hurried back to Tom.

But there was no change. When he'd unsaddled the mule and unrolled Tom's bedroll, he found a tin of peaches, one of hardtack, and a small corked bitters bottle. He unstoppered it and, after smelling it, discovered it not to be bitters, but whiskey. *A little touch for the trail,* Tom had told him he always brought along. The peaches and biscuits would do for dinner for the both of them, if he could get Tom to take any nourishment, and the cans and bottle would come in handy in the days ahead. As would the rest of the grub.

He busied himself, making a fire and gathering wood until he had a pile that would last for three days. Tom had the makings, and a few sulfur matches in his tobacco bag, so the fire came easy.

Somewhere high above in the darkness there must have been an opening, as the smoke did not fill the cavern down to the high end of the rift, but rather disappeared upward. *When I get Tom back to right, I'll need to explore and find where that smoke's getting out,* Roan thought. *We need a back way out of here.*

But there was much to do first.

Chapter 10

Skeeter McKelvie and Poker Pete Howard had heard some distant shots as they climbed up and around the west side of the mountain. But they were so distant they had no idea where they came from. It could have been Tom, Roan, and Slim John shooting at a bear or wolf, or even a cougar. Or it could have been Bar X riders doing the same. Then, of course, it could have been Bar X riders throwing some warning shots at the Lucky Seven riders, as they'd been prone to do the last few months.

They'd reached the top of Deep Creek Gulch, and visually searched the other side of the canyon for Tom and the others to no avail. After waiting over an hour, they decided to drive their side of the canyon even if the others had been detained for some reason.

They did so, gathering four wild and rank cows and five calves, reaching the bottom and the assigned meeting place where the creek flowed into the Little

Blackfoot River. Again they waited over an hour.

Skeeter, never known for his patience, finally said to hell with the others. Tom had the grub tied to the back of his saddle, and if he didn't get there they'd spend a cold and hungry night alone. There was a corral at an old line camp not an hour downriver, so they decided to drive the cattle there, pen them, then go on back around the mountain to the ranch. It would mean they'd arrive well after dark, but it was better than holing up there without grub and, more importantly, morning coffee.

Badger and Slater followed Roan's track all the way back to the ranch house, arriving there not long after Roan had ridden away. They were surprised to see the house in flames.

They were hailed from the barn as they got into shouting range. It was Givens. They entered the barn to find Blodget moaning in a pile of hay, his pants leg cut away and a blood-soaked rag tied around his calf.

"What the hell happened here?" Badger demanded.

"Woman or the boy shot a big ol' chunk out of Blodget's leg," Givens said.

"What was you two doing here?" Badger said, his face beginning to redden.

"Why, doin' what you said we should do. Shootin' down Lucky Seven hands."

Givens was standing in the middle of the barn, his Winchester hanging loose at his side. He had no chance to raise it as Badger stepped forward and brought his own rifle across the side of Givens's head. He fell in a heap. Badger kicked his rifle aside, then clubbed him two more times as he crawled away and found some protection behind Blodget.

"You damn stupid fool. You're worthless as a bucket of spit. I told you we was riding up the mountain to pick off those old boys. You only came here because of the woman."

"Woman's dead," Givens said, rubbing the ugly welt beginning to rise into a knot on the side of his head. "So's the blacksmith . . . Coppersmith. We got him right off."

"In the fire?" Badger asked.

"No. I shot the blacksmith and Blodget shot the woman down. He's in the tack room and she's up the hill a ways."

"And the boy?"

"He came and went," Givens said, shrugging.

"He came and went and you and this fool let him?"

"He snuck up on us like a skunk in the henhouse."

Badger tried to circle Blodget to get at Givens, but Givens kept the wounded man between them, scrambling around on all fours.

"This does no good," Slater said.

"Hell," Badger snapped at him, "you're shot, Blodget is shot, Givens is dumb as that barn door. And we still got three or four of them out there."

"You didn't get the others?" Givens asked, his tone condemning.

"We shot one dead," Slater offered, "and shot one down, probably dead. We were following the boy here. . . ."

"So there's still at least three of them out there?" Givens said, cautiously getting to his feet.

"Yeah, and you ain't going nowhere until we get them."

"They'll come back here," Givens said. "All but the boy. He knows we're here."

"Maybe," Badger said, scratching his head. "Get the horses in the barn. We'll hole up here and wait till the sun's high tomorrow. If no one shows, we'll ride out and hunt the mountain tomorrow."

"What about Blodget?" Givens asked.

Blodget raised his head. "I'm shot good. Damn kid blew a chunk outta my leg bigger'n your fist. It ain't never gonna be right again. I ain't riding up no mountain."

"Damn fool," Badger said. "If we have to ride up the mountain, we'll put you on your horse and head you out to the Bar X."

"Don't know if I can make it."

"Then, Blodget, you won't make it."

"Bastard," Blodget said in a low voice, but Badger ignored him.

"Get the horses inside. You two get in the hayloft, one front, one back. We'll wait."

As the sun dropped below the Flint Range to the west, Bert Prager sat on his front porch in a bentwood rocker. His ramrod, Kelly Dugan, a tall man, well over six feet, stood on the steps of the wide porch. The house was two stories, with a big extra-wide front door, an entry hall, parlors off both sides of the entrance, and over twenty rooms. It was the finest house west of Butte. Prager had built it for his second wife, but she'd run off, and since his son had been killed, he lived in the big house alone, except for Elga, a fat Norwegian housekeeper.

"I didn't think he'd never sell," Dugan said, shaking his head in wonder.

"It's a good thing I got it bought when I did," Prager said, quietly rocking. Prager packed a corncob pipe as he spoke. "McKeag was shot down like the dog he was — in the alley beside the Bonny Glen right before I rode out of town."

"The hell you say? Dan McKeag? How did that happen?"

"Some woman, the way I heard it. Some bar girl."

"They gonna hang her?"

Bert smiled, then lit the pipe and blew a long stream of smoke. "Hell, she run off. Doubt if they'll ever catch her. Let it be a lesson, Kelly. Don't mess about on your wife."

Kelly shrugged, changing the subject as he was uncomfortable and saddened with the thought Dan McKeag was doing something he shouldn't in that regard, and taken aback by the thought of McKeag's death. "So, when are we taking over the Lucky Seven?"

Kelly Dugan was a cattleman. He tried hard to keep out of the politics of the Bar X. All he wanted was to push his men, raise, brand, round up, and drive cattle. And that was the way Bert Prager said he

123

wanted it. Dugan had been on the Bar X for a dozen years, and been ramrod for half that time.

"We already have taken over," Prager said.

"Maybe I should ride over there?" Dugan asked.

"Nope. You're gonna ramrod that spread too, but not until things settle down a mite. I sent those old boys who was here yesterday. They are gonna make sure that worthless Lucky Seven bunch has left."

Dugan was suspicious of this, but knew better than to ask. "You got the stock in the deal?"

"I did."

"Must be seven — eight hundred head on the Lucky Seven. We're gonna need more hands — and those four didn't look like cowmen to me."

"They ain't. They'll be riding on when this little job is done. You ride into town tomorrow, after you get the men to work. Take Meegan and make a day of it. Take my buggy. And see who you can hire. Four more should do it."

"Yes, sir." Dugan touched his hat and spun and walked away toward his little cabin next to the bunkhouse. He'd known Dan McKeag for many years, and it saddened him to hear that the man was shot down. McKeag, in spite of his trouble with the Bar X, was a good man. Meegan, Kelly's wife, would be saddened to hear of his passing. She'd begun to make friends with Erin McKeag when they'd met in town at social functions, friends at least until the real trouble had started between the ranches.

Dugan couldn't help but wonder about the mission of the four men he'd seen meeting with Prager just the day before. He knew one of the men slightly. Al Givens had spent some time in Deer Lodge City, visiting with some old boy who was doing time at the Montana Territorial Prison, the penitentiary as it was known locally, the main reason for the town's existence. Kelly knew that Givens was no cowman; in fact, he thought the man a bit of an owlhoot. They'd only talked a couple of times at Tidwell's Saloon. That had been enough for Kelly. No, those four were up to no good, and Prager was behind it. Damn, why couldn't the man just tend to his cattle and the Bar X? It was big enough for any man, but Kelly knew that Prager would probably never be satisfied — not until he owned every grazing acre in Montana Territory. He even had eyes on the giant Conrad Kohrs spread on the south side of the valley.

Kelly girded himself as he entered the cabin. Meegan, his buxom large-boned wife, was sitting in her rocker, mending, when he walked in. The rocker had embroidered horsehair cushions, and tatted doilies adorned the tables and shelves in the room. A framed sampler hanging on the log wall offered the hopeful message "Home Sweet Home." The little two-room cabin was clean as the proverbial pin.

"Did you brush your trousers off and scrape your boots?"

"Yes, ma'am," Dugan said, then cleared his throat. "I got some bad news."

He related the story of Dan McKeag being shot down in Helena.

"I'm going over there tomorrow," Meegan said. "Erin will be beside herself and will need some womenfolk around."

"Prager won't have it, Meegan. You'll stay right here."

"That's not right, Kelly Dugan."

"Right or wrong, there's been too much trouble, 'twixt us and the Lucky Seven. Prager will give me the boot, you go over there — besides, they're all gone. Prager bought them out, right before McKeag was killed. That's what he was doing in Helena."

"That's a pile of bull dung and you know it, Kelly. McKeag would never sell. Besides, if that rotten old man did fire you, it would be the best thing that ever happened to us."

Kelly ignored her slight against the boss. "That's not what Bert said, just now over on the porch of the big house. Bert Prager is the new owner of the Lucky Seven."

"And I'm Queen Victoria. There's something amiss here, Kelly."

"Not my affair, Meegan, nor your'n. You mend and tend the place and raise up little Kel; I'll grow stock, and we'll do fine. Let Prager worry about the politickin' and getting us our draft every month."

Meegan stood and headed for the small bedroom in the back of the house that they shared with their three-year-old son Kelly Jr. She stopped in the doorway. "It ain't right, Kelly. Something's amiss here. I should go over. . . ."

"I told you." His voice rose an octave, something that hadn't happened twice since they'd been married, five years before. "You can't go over there. Prager has a crew there making sure things are ready for our hands."

She looked at him sadly, shaking her head. "Sometimes, Kelly Dugan, you've got to stand up for what's right, and this doesn't smell right to me."

"Minding our own affairs is what's right, Mrs. Dugan. You go on to bed. I'll be along in a while."

Kelly sat in the rocker and packed his pipe. He tried to get his mind on what it would require, running the new place, but his mind kept coming back to the McKeags.

It was a sad day.

Kelly walked over to a shelf and retrieved one of his prized possessions, an old frayed copy of *Gulliver's Travels* by Jonathan Swift. A half-dozen books adorned the shelf, mostly Irish poets, but they made him think too much to sleep. Gulliver's adventures would quiet him.

He needed something to help him sleep, to keep his mind on cattle and off Dan and Erin McKeag, and at Meegan's insistence he'd given up demon liquor years ago.

Chapter 11

It was good and dark, with the moon not up yet, when Skeeter McKelvie and Poker Pete Howard rode over the last hill on their way back to the Lucky Seven home place, driving a dozen head of cows and calves ahead of them. They'd decided not to pen them, as the corral had no water and little feed. Skeeter looked down at where he was sure the group of buildings should be. No lights shone in the windows, which was not unusual this time of night, but the glow of embers and occasional lick of flame arose from where it seemed the ranch house should have stood.

"What the devil is that?" he asked Pete.

"Don't look good."

"You don't suppose —"

"Let's get down there." Pete whipped up his horse, with Skeeter close behind, leaving the cattle on their own.

In moments, they pounded into the yard and slid to a halt up by the well.

"By all that's holy," Skeeter said,

sweeping his hat off as he dismounted, "the damned house done burned to the ground."

"Mrs. McKeag! Cookie!" Pete called out, then dismounted. "Where the hell is everybody?" He walked over to where he could see into the corral beside the barn, then called back. "No one here a'tall. The others aren't back."

"Let's rub these horses down," Skeeter said, then his voice dropped. "Then make sure there's no one in that pile of rubble, if'n it's cool enough to move about."

Both of them unsaddled and carried their gear to the tack room. Skeeter kicked the door open, and Pete followed him in.

"Damn, it's dark," Skeeter said, trying to find his way across the room.

"I can see you fine, and you're Lucky Seven riders?" the voice rang out from the doorway into the barn.

"Yeah, who's there?"

"And it's a piss-poor sight to behold."

"Who — ?" Skeeter didn't get it out. Flame roared out of the doorway and he was blown across the room, a chest full of buckshot, to fall next to the body of Simon Coppersmith. His gear tumbled away.

Pete didn't wait to see who the shooter was, but dropped his gear and dove out the door, slapping for his revolver as he did so.

Badger had called the boys down from the loft, sending Givens and Slater outside and around the barn when they'd heard the two Lucky Seven riders pound into the yard. He'd waited near the doorway for them to enter, as he figured they'd be putting up their tack.

Givens and Slater met Pete as he dove back out of the tack room, both of them firing their side arms several times before Pete could draw his weapon.

"Rotten low — lifes —" was all he managed to get out before he quieted, with a wheezing sigh, three holes pumping blood from his chest.

Badger walked slowly out of the tack room, closely eyeing the still body of the second Lucky Seven rider. "Drag the three of them up the hill by the woman. You can plant them up there in the morning."

"And we'll be diggin' that rocky ground while you're having your coffee?" Slater asked, his tone sour. He was very, very sorry he'd holstered his revolver.

"Yep, while I'm having my coffee, or taking a piss, or doing whatever the hell I want to be doing," Badger said, then spit a wad of chewing tobacco onto Poker Pete's bloody chest, but only glancing down for half a heartbeat. "If'n you don't like it, you can draw that hogleg and try to get a shot off afore your guts decorate the dirt." But he had the shotgun leveled on Slater's midsection.

"Not tonight," Slater said. "Not tonight."

"Anytime you say. Now drag. We're sleeping in the barn, and I don't want them stinking up the place."

Slater and Givens each grabbed one of Pete's ankles and began to drag.

The following afternoon, Paddy Dundee rode over the mountain to the foothill valley where the Lucky Seven buildings lay. From the distance, he was shocked to see the house a pile of burnt logs, the fireplace standing forlorn and alone. As he neared at a canter, he could see the embers still smoking.

It took him only moments to determine that no one was about, then to locate four unmarked graves just up the hillside behind the destroyed house.

He stood in wonder, staring at the graves, praying that his sister was not among them. What in the world had happened? Were they killed in the fire?

He had to find out, and the only way he

knew to do so was to ride into Deer Lodge City and look up the deputy marshal.

It took him until nightfall to reach town. Then he found he had to ride up Tin Cap Joe Creek, another three miles, to where the marshal kept a small spread. He did learn at the general store that Houston Greenlaw was the marshal's name and where he lived. He passed the formidable stone penitentiary on the way out of the little town. Its thick stone walls rose at least thirty feet in the air, and the turrets at its corners even higher. The building was well over a hundred paces long and more than half that depth. A guard at the heavy iron front door waved at him as he passed. Pad tipped his derby at the guard, happy that he wasn't one of the guard's wards.

Just as the last light faded in the west, Pad reined up at a rail fence in front of a small house with a porch all the way across its front. A pair of black-and-tan hounds bolted out from under the porch, barking like the devil but wagging their tails as Pad dismounted.

By the time his foot hit the dirt, the door was open. "Can I help you?" a voice called out from the heavy-girthed man standing in the doorway, backlit by a bright room.

"I hope so," Pad said. He hesitated before opening the gate to a slat fence that surrounded the yard. "The dogs all right?" he asked.

"They're wagging their tails," the man said.

"It ain't the tail end that bites," Pad said.

The man laughed. "True enough. Come on in."

Pad beat the trail dust off his pants with the narrow-brimmed derby hat he'd taken off one of the toughs they'd shot down in the Bonny Glen, then stepped forward and took the man's offered hand. "I'm Paddy Dundee, from over Helena way."

"Houston Greenlaw," the salt-and-pepper-haired man offered. "You might be looking for the marshal?"

"Yes, sir, I would be."

"Then come on in, I'm him, and the marshal and his wife will buy you a cup of coffee. You look as if you could use it."

After Pad met Mrs. Greenlaw, who was even more gray-haired than the marshal — Anne he was told to call her — he was seated at the dinner table while the silver-haired lady poured him a cup, then cleared the table.

"Now, sir, what can I do for you?" Greenlaw asked.

"You know the McKeags?"

"I know Dan McKeag well, and consider him a friend."

"Then you know what happened out at the Lucky Seven?"

"I know what was reported earlier today. A terrible thing, the house burned and Mrs. McKeag and three of their hands were killed."

"My God," Paddy said. He'd still hoped against hope that Erin didn't occupy one of the graves. He collected himself, quelling the burning in the back of his throat, then asked, "And who was it reported this fire?"

"One of the Bar X hands . . . the Bar X is the ranch next to the Lucky Seven. He was riding through today — fellow name of Givens — and he reported it. Said he and a couple of other Bar X hands were over there checking on the place — seems the Lucky Seven was lately purchased by the Bar X, which came as a hell of a surprise to me — anyway, they were over that way and saw the remains of the fire and those that were burned up. In fact, it was Givens and the Bar X hands that buried them. Must have happened at night, as all of them were caught unawares."

"In the house? You think the hands were sleeping in the house?"

"No, fact is, I don't." Greenlaw took a long draw on his coffee mug, studying Pad as he did so. "That's only one of the things about the report from Givens that didn't set well with me." Greenlaw rose and walked to a window, his coffee cup in hand. He turned back to Pad. "What's your interest in this, Mr. Dundee?"

"Pad, if you would, sir. Erin McKeag is . . . was . . . my sister."

"I'm sorry, sir. This has been a very bad few days for you. Dan McKeag killed in Helena, then this tragic fire." The marshal studied Pad as he spoke.

Pad hesitated telling Greenlaw that Dan was still alive. No telling to whom the marshal owed his allegiance. Dan would let it be known he was alive when he was ready. Pad changed the subject.

"How about Roan, the nephew, and the other hands?"

"I have no idea. Givens said nothing about the rest of them."

"So," Pad said, "are you going out there to investigate?"

"I am. First light."

"Then if you don't mind, I'll ride back out there with you. I'm heading back to Helena first thing."

"I've got a fine hayloft in the barn, if

136

you'd like to sleep over. Feel free to hay and grain Dan's horse."

Pad hesitated a moment. "You've a good eye for horseflesh, Marshal," Pad said without further explanation. "Obliged, for the coffee and the hayloft."

"I'll give you a yell before sunup, and you can join us for breakfast."

"Obliged again, Marshal Greenlaw."

"Houston, remember. You get some supper?"

"I bought me a handful of jerky and hardtack in town when I passed the general store. I'm fine, thanks."

"In the morning then." Pad headed for the door, but Greenlaw stopped him with a comment before he could exit. "Sorry about your sister, Pad. Your brother-in-law and sister were gentlefolk and fine friends of mine and the missus. I do plan to find out what happened out there."

Pad nodded, placated at least for the moment, then headed out to the barn.

While Pad was having coffee with the marshal at Bogart's Café in Deer Lodge — the marshal wanted to stop to make sure Givens was not still in town — Bert Prager had just returned from town, and was meeting with Badger, Givens, Slater, and

Blodget. Blodget was seated in Prager's rocking chair on the front porch, his leg bandaged and propped up on the porch rail. Prager sat alone in a two-person swing hung with rope from the porch roof. The other three men stood nearby. Elga, the housekeeper, waddled through the front door, her blond hair askew, wearing a stained apron and carrying a tray. She offered each of them a small glass of whiskey. Blodget downed his in one swig, handing the glass back to her.

"Thank you. Another, I need it."

"Later," Prager snapped. "We got business first."

"My leg feels like it's on fire. Whiskey would —"

"Later." Prager yelled over his shoulder at Elga, who stood just inside the door. "Woman, get that bottle of Doc Hostettler's I just bought." He turned back to Blodget. "You shouldn't a went and got yerself shot all to hell." His eyes scanned all of them, and the question was directed to the group. "So, none of them boys wanted to join up with the Bar X. You had to shoot 'em all down . . . as well as the woman?"

Badger spoke quickly. "Hell, Prager, they all shot at us, including the woman. It was self-defense. All of 'em is buried deep.

Won't be anybody figuring out what we was up to."

Prager pulled a small sack from his shirt pocket, took out a pinch of tobacco, and stuffed it behind his lower lip. "So, that's how it was . . . they was shootin' at you?" Prager shook his head, wanting to believe, although he had his doubts. What he didn't doubt was what Badger had done afterward. "That's only part of it, Badger. What the devil do you think you were doing, sending Givens in to make a report to the marshal? Greenlaw jumped me in town early this morning, an' I had to play dumb as a dead dog. Good thing was he thinks it was a fire that killed all of them."

Badger got a slow smile. Prager waited patiently for him. "What makes you think *I* sent him?" Badger finally said.

While he was speaking, Elga crossed the porch and handed the bottle of bitters to Blodget, who drank it down, then looked as if he was going to splatter the floor with his lunch. As Elga returned inside, he mumbled, "That poison ain't gonna help."

Prager ignored him, still in Badger's face. "You sent him . . . you seem to ramrod this bunch of no-accounts." He spit a stream of tobacco juice, trying to clear the porch, but it splattered on the boards.

"I thunk it important the marshal knew there was a fire — and it was the natural thing to do — report it. Makes us look innocent as newborns." Badger laughed. "Besides, I'd think you'd want us to act like good neighbors." He guffawed at that.

"And," Prager added, a slow smile coming to his own face, "important he knew you fellas was working for me when that fire happened and all those folks died?"

Again Badger gave him the slow smile. "Now, that's a thought. Thataway you won't be trying to put it on us. It's probably a good idea you pay us up so we can be on our way."

"That's one thing you're right about."

Badger reiterated his logic. "Now that the marshal knows we was working for you, it ain't likely you'll have him come after us, claiming we was acting on our own."

Prager rose to his feet. "You know, Badger, I don't much like clever men, particularly no-account fools who think they're clever. Fact is, I think you're so dumb you couldn't teach a hen to cluck. But it's no matter, as you're on your way out of the territory."

Badger's face reddened.

"So I'm gonna tell you this only one time. You'll get your money, then you four are gonna ride out — and I mean far out of the territory. I don't want to hear about you ever, not ever again. You'll die in your boots if'n I do. Right now you're near enough to hell to smell the smoke and hear the sizzle."

Badger guffawed. "And I'm harder than the hubs of hell, and you'd best remember that, old man. I'm heading for California," Badger said, his tone still a little superior. "We'll all be out of the territory soon as horseflesh can get us there."

"Do that, and don't never, never come back." Prager's eyes scanned the other three. "None of you."

"You should know," Badger said, "that we all agree, should the law come after us, we'll let it be known it was Bert Prager and the Bar X what hired us."

"Yeah, you're fine hands, riding for the brand." He laughed sardonically, then his tone hardened. "And you should know, Badger, that I can hire another hundred men to hunt you down and split all yer gullets, should you ever be seen in this country again." Prager scanned them again with hard eyes, letting each of them know he spoke in earnest. Then with great effort,

141

he rose to his feet, again spat a stream of tobacco juice, and said, "I'll get your money, then you move like turpentined cats."

"I ain't scared of no hundred men," Badger said as Prager limped with his cane through the door. His voice rang out behind the old rancher. "I'd fight a three-foot round saw and give it a dozen rotations — no damn thousand men scare me!"

There was dead silence on the porch for many minutes, until Prager gimped back out and paid them off, remaining standing until they were mounted.

"I got to get to town to see the doc," Blodget moaned as he was hoisted into the saddle by Slater and Givens.

"The hell you say," Prager snapped. "The next doctor's the other side of Hell Gate. You can see him there. And you'll tell him you were a clumsy fool who dropped yer weapon and it went off — accidental-like."

"That's three or four days' ridin'. I got to go —"

"Shudup," Badger snapped, "or I'll shoot you where you'll be stone dead and won't have to worry about whining like no woman. You're too old to suck and too young to die. You're gonna live to see the elephant again. Now tighten the latigo on yer jaw, I'm tired of hearin' you."

"I'll die in the saddle anyways."

"Then die," Prager snapped. "Now y'all get on down the road."

Badger gave him a salute and a slow smile, spun the horse, and led the others off toward a glowing sunset.

Prager yelled at his housekeeper as the four rode out, "Elga, get yer fat backside movin' and bring me a slug of good whiskey from the decanter on the sideboard."

He took a seat in the rocker, slowly rocking until she appeared with the glass.

He nodded at her, then toasted the sunset. "It's a fine evening, a very, very fine evening."

He leaned back in the chair and lit a store-bought cigar. Very pleased with himself, he thought of the money he would make in the coming years. The Northern Pacific Railroad would be coming through in the next few years, and timber from McKeag's Mountain would supply them with ties and stringers for trestles. But there was more, there was that one great commodity that had built the territory — gold. Gold that those fools, the McKeags, had no idea was located on the Lucky

Seven. Now it was Prager's, all his. He day-dreamed of the ranches he would buy. Hell, he might even buy out Old Man Kohrs.

But an hour later the evening, and his quiet revelry, were marred by an unexpected visit.

Just at full dark, with Bert Prager still rocking contentedly on the porch smoking his corncob pipe, a rider reined up at the hitching rail. Prager, slightly in his cups from four glasses of whiskey, yelled, "Who the hell's there?"

"Bert, it's Houston."

Prager was slightly taken aback. He hadn't thought to see the Deer Lodge City area deputy marshal quite so soon. But he collected himself. "Come on up on the porch, Houston. Elga," he yelled over his shoulder, "bring that decanter of good whiskey and another glass."

Houston crossed the wide front yard and mounted the steps. "I could use it, Bert. It's been a long day."

"You still chasing those robbers that got the stage?"

Houston studied him carefully. "Yep, but it's that fire out at the Lucky Seven that's got me worked up at the moment."

Prager chewed on that a moment as Elga

144

brought out the whiskey and poured a generous one for the marshal and topped off Prager's glass. Prager decided to change the subject. "Who was that riding with you this morning?"

"Old friend from Helena."

"Oh. Anyone I should know?"

"Nope." It was obvious the marshal was not going to be verbose about his riding mate.

"So, what else is new?"

"Is Al Givens about?"

"Nope. Quit. Trying to get work out of that boy and his cohorts was useless as sitting a milk bucket under a bull. Rode out for Denver earlier." He didn't want to be specific about the time, for if Greenlaw knew the four hired guns had ridden out only an hour or so ahead of his arriving, he might go after them. And he was a good enough tracker to find their trail west, not south. Greenlaw was a bulldog, and Prager knew it, and feared the fact that he never kowtowed to Prager's pot of gold.

"Denver? You sure?"

"Only know what he said. Why?"

"It seems he lied about Erin McKeag and those other three graves out at the fire."

"The hell. Why would he lie?"

"You tell me."

Prager slugged down the remaining three fingers of whiskey and reached for the decanter, which Elga had left. He poured another glass for himself, and motioned to Greenlaw, but he refused.

Greenlaw didn't let it go. "So, you've bought the Lucky Seven?"

"I did."

"It would soothe me a mite if you'd show me the deed."

Prager's brow furrowed. "You doubtin' my word, Greenlaw?"

"Just doing my job, Mr. Prager. Sometimes it riles folks, but it's my job. And everybody knows there was bad blood between the Bar X and the Lucky Seven. The deed?"

Prager shook his head in disgust. "Elga, bring me the iron box — under my desk."

While they waited, Prager packed and lit his corncob. Nothing more was said until she exited the door, lugging a small but obviously heavy load, and set the box at Prager's feet. He fished a ring of keys out of his pocket, opened the padlock, shuffled though some papers, and came out with a folded one.

"Here," he said, a triumphant tone in his voice. He handed over the document.

Greenlaw unfolded it, then had to walk

over and open the door to read by the light of the oil lamps in the entry. He returned and handed it back. "Looks sound to me."

"Right as rain in a dry August. Did you see who witnessed it?"

"I did. Judge Harley."

"Territorial Judge Oscar Pettibone Harley, appointed to that post by our fine departed President Abraham Lincoln. That ought to be good enough for God in heaven . . . is it good enough for you?"

Greenlaw sighed deeply. "Those folks over there at the Lucky Seven were all shot full of holes, Bert. I've got a multiple murder on my hands — a heinous crime. Worse, the others are all missing. No one's about."

Prager merely shrugged his shoulders. "I already said a prayer for the lot of them." He yawned, then offered, "All I know is I sent some men over there to check on things, and they found the place burned down. I would have thought the McKeags did it out of spite after I bought the place, had my men not come back and reported the fire and the dead folk."

"Your men buried them. That's what Givens said. Any of the rest of those men about?"

"They rode in as a bunch, and quit as a

bunch. All rode out together." Prager had finished his pipe, and pounded the ash out onto the porch.

Greenlaw rose. "Thanks for the drink. If you hear anything about where they went, let me know."

"The drink's my pleasure, Houston, but I told you, they rode out saying they was headin' for Denver."

The marshal nodded his head, but Prager could see he didn't believe a word he said about where the four were headed. Greenlaw turned and started down the stairs, but Prager stopped him. "Houston, we're butcherin' hogs down in the bottoms tomorrow. You want I should send the missus over a side? It would surely be my pleasure."

Greenlaw eyed the rich cattleman carefully before he answered. "Bert, you send us a smoked ham at Christmas, like always, and I'll send you over a bottle of good brandy. Best we leave it at that."

Prager again shrugged his shoulders. "Ride careful. Moon won't be up for a while." Greenlaw was halfway to his horse when Prager again shouted after him. "And Houston, let it be known that I'm looking for hands — hewers and sawyers, and boys who don't mind grubbing with a shovel."

"New project, Bert?"

"Yep. Building a ditch. Surveyors are on their way."

Greenlaw waved over his shoulder, mounted, and disappeared into the night.

Chapter 12

The next day, late in the afternoon, Pad reined up in front of the Bonny Glen. He'd ridden most of the night before. He dismounted slowly. He was exhausted. Not so much physically, as mentally. He'd ridden all the way trying to figure the best way to tell Dan that his wife was dead, his cowhands dead or missing. And almost as bad, Dan's young nephew — where was Roan?

The reason the trip home had taken most of the night and all this day was that Marshal Houston Greenlaw had insisted they open the graves, see who they held, then properly mark them. Over each grave, Greenlaw said a few words. Over Erin's, he recited the Lord's Prayer and the complete Twenty-first Psalm.

Pad had thought he was beyond crying, but he learned differently as they again filled her grave, after carefully, but quickly, building a coffin from barn siding and laying her body on a cushion of saddle blankets. The rest of them had to make do being rolled in saddle blankets.

He and Greenlaw learned one thing for sure; none of the victims had died in a fire.

The Bar X hand, Givens, had been lying.

Pad passed Toby, the swamper, who was back at work, waved at Tarbell, the bartender, and not seeing Rose Ballard in the saloon, walked straight to the stairway at the rear of the place.

"Miss Rose ain't up there," Tarbell shouted at him across the room, but he ignored the man and took the stairs two at a time.

Dan was sitting on the edge of the day bed made up in the parlor.

"You trying to get up again?" Pad said.

"And a good day to you too, Pad Dundee. Where's Erin?"

Pad took a deep breath, and stood, bowler hat in both hands in front of him. "Dan, Erin's gone."

"Gone. Gone where?"

"She's gone, Dan. Gone to meet the maker."

Dan's eyes grew wide, and he lurched to his feet and took two stumbling steps toward Pad.

"No!" he shouted, then fell forward.

Pad caught him, but Dan collapsed in his arms. Pad carried him, his arms wrapped tightly around Dan's chest, Dan silently withering in his arms, to the bed, and gently laid him down.

Dan lay there for several moments, both hands covering his face. Finally, he pulled them away, and stared at Pad for a moment through reddened eyes.

"What . . . Pad . . . what took her?"

"The house burned, Dan. But it wasn't that. I went to the ranch, and found the house in ashes and four fresh graves —"

"Four?"

"Let me finish. I found four graves and no one about. I rode straight into town and out to the marshal's. Greenlaw and I went back out there, early yesterday."

"Pad, it can't be her."

"It was her, Dan. We opened the graves. I argued against it — for my own sake, I'm afraid. But Greenlaw wouldn't have it any other way. It was Erin, shot through the chest, and three of your hands. . . ."

"Shot?"

"Through the chest. Marshal Greenlaw knew two of the others, hands of yours, and thought the third one was also."

"I knew something was bad wrong when she didn't come. And . . ." Dan's voice caught, and he had to wait a moment before continuing. "And Roan?"

"No sign of young Roan, or the other hands. I wanted to look around some more, Dan, but I figured I'd better get back here first. I lit a shuck out of there and rode the night through."

"Tom. My ramrod. A black man. Was Tom one of the three?"

"White men all. One a big fella with a full beard —"

"Real big?

"He'd take first prize at a bull show, were he still on his feet."

"Simon. Simon Coppersmith."

"Center-shot twice. And the other two shot also . . . One of them was a little fella, no bigger'n some fourteen-year-olds I've seen, but he was old."

"Skeeter." Dan sat up in bed, his look hardening. "Get a horse for yourself. We're going out there."

"You can't, Dan. Not yet."

Rose Ballard was standing in the doorway at the top of the stairs. "Can't what?" she asked.

"Dan wants to go to the ranch."

"And I *am* going," Dan said adamantly.

"You're not going anywhere, Dan," Rose said. "A week, maybe two."

"I have to go." His blue eyes turned cold as ice as he said it.

"And if Prager finds you're back?" she asked. "You won't do anyone any good if you're dead yourself."

"My wife's dead. Some of my hands are dead. I don't know where — no one knows where my nephew is — or my ramrod — a man who's been like a father to me since my own was taken. I have to go back now."

"My God," Rose said, taken aback, raising a hand over her mouth, then letting it slowly drop away. "I am so very sorry."

Paddy looked at her and shrugged his shoulders. "I can hire a wagon . . . make a bed in the back."

"I have a buggy, a wagon really, a phaeton. I just had the top redone and side curtains made. With a fine pair of matched grays smooth as churned butter. It's got a backseat but we can remove it, and make a bed for Dan in the back. It'll take two full days on the Mullen Road, but they'll make it easy. But that doesn't solve the problem of Prager and his men."

"I've *got* to go," Dan said icily in a manner that left no doubt he meant it, if he had to walk.

"I'll make you a deal," Pad said. "I'll get us on the road, in, say, three or four days —"

"Tomorrow, no longer. Or I'll damn well take Dancer and ride."

"You know, Dan McKeag," Rose said, stepping forward, "I understand this is a terrible shock to you. I understand that. But for a man who's been accepting my hospitality for almost two weeks, who's wanting to borrow my pride and joy, my wagon and team, and who should be bedridden for another two weeks, if Doc Gallagher knows anything, you're mighty insistent about getting your way. Muleheaded, in fact. And you're talking to a man who just rode five hard days and all night on your account."

"I have to —"

"I know what you have to do, and I appreciate it and even admire you for it. But you can't help the dead, particularly if you're dead yourself. And you will be if you go off half-cocked . . . Prager won't have to have you shot down. After three more nights' sleep you can borrow my wagon, not until then. Ride your damn horse and die in the saddle, if you think that'll help your nephew."

"My nephew is missing . . . I can't just . . ."

"And Pad and I will help you find him. Three days hence."

155

Dan sighed deeply. "Get her fancy rig ready," he said to Pad. "Now," he proclaimed to both of them, "if you don't mind, I need to be by myself for a while."

"That I understand," Rose said, her voice soft as a feather. She spun on her heel, dragging Pad out behind her. She hesitated at the door. "We'll leave before dawn, after you've slept three more nights."

"We?" Dan said, but she slammed the door behind them.

Dan lay back down. A tingle of anger crept slowly across his chest, moving aside a tiny iota of the grief. Over the next three days it supplanted a good deal of the grief, burning deep, silent, and ominous, like an ember from his destroyed home, sizzling deep in his chest.

His first piece of business, after he'd made Tom comfortable and taken care of the horses, was to ride back and bury Slim John. It was not a pleasant task, as the forest critters had been at him. As soon as Tom was well enough to leave alone for several hours, Roan planned to ride back to the ranch and bury his aunt and Simon — if no one had yet found them. He hoped they had, as it was a job he loathed.

A fat whitetail doe hung in the rear of the cave where it was cool. Strips cut from her side meat and flanks were on a willow frame near the fire, drying for jerky and preservation. The horses had been moved daily to new graze, but still in reach of the little stream. Roan had been busy. Making the cave livable had been a good part of it. He'd spent three days tending Tom, who had awakened, but for the first day was delirious. The second, he began to make sense, and took broth made from venison, laced and thickened with smashed beans from the food bag. By the third day, Tom seemed to be mending well. And he was making sense.

Even so, Roan was frustrated. He'd been working on the shattered stock of the Sharps, smoothing the hole with his folding knife, carving a filler for the hole shot in the stock. He carved the root-knee of a downed tamarack to make the plug, probably harder than the original stock. He used sap from a nearby pine, weeping from where it had lost a branch to the wind, to set the plug until he could find some real glue. Simon had some milk glue in the tack room, glue Erin had made.

These were not the reasons for his frustrations. The reason was he could not yet put the Sharps to work hunting Bar X riders, avenging his aunt and friends. His stomach stayed knotted most times with a burning desire to avenge his aunt and friend Simon . . . and Tom, who he knew might still die. But he doubted it. Only this afternoon, Tom had complained that they couldn't play Pedro, but the card game required four players, so he had to satisfy himself with solitaire. Roan had tried to keep the news of Erin's death from Tom, but couldn't, as Tom immediately insisted that Roan ride back to the ranch for help. Erin had been a favorite of Tom's, and he took it almost as badly as Roan had.

But Roan, despite his frustrations, kept busy.

Revenge could wait, but it would come. As sure as God had dictated that the sun rise in the east.

Before dawn the third day, Rose and Paddy carefully loaded Dan and some camp gear into the back of her phaeton, and Paddy took the traces. By mid-morning, with the strong grays, they were nearing the top of Hell Gate Pass.

Dan had argued, unsuccessfully, that Rose shouldn't go, and she had countered that he could always ride his blood gelding,

Dancer, if he didn't want her along. He was learning that she was a woman to be cajoled, not argued with.

Dancer was tied to the back of the phaeton, and Blue trotted along beside him, occasionally chasing a grouse off the trail, or following a rabbit's scent into the underbrush.

Dan had managed only a few steps, and was still incapacitated to the point that he was almost helpless. The shot to his upper right chest had affected the strength in his right arm, but that was a good trade for the bullet missing his heart. The thing that worried him most was the fact he was right-handed, and his weakness would affect almost everything he did . . . including firing his side arm. So far, he could barely lift it.

He spent a good part of the way lifting and sighting his revolver with his left hand. He'd done it a thousand times before when he unloaded its .44-40 cartridges, and now began not only lifting and sighting, but cocking it.

He knew he was going to have use for it.

Chapter 13

It was late in the afternoon, while he was heading over to restake the horses, when Roan saw the riders working their way up the mountain. They were still a half mile or more away. Instead of restaking the animals as he'd planned, Roan led them back to the cave and deep inside where he could tie the picket line between two stalagmites, and where they wouldn't be heard if someone passed close to the cave entrance.

Then he returned to the main cavern, gathering up the Sharps and a handful of shells. Tom, now sitting up, eyed the boy carefully, and spoke up as Roan headed for the outside.

"Roan, what are you up to?"

"There's riders coming up the other side of the canyon, over by the creek."

"So. Let them pass. They won't find us here."

"I got to see who they are, Tom."

"How many?"

"Four or five."

"You'd do best to stay here."

"Can't see who they are if'n I stay here. It might be Uncle Dan and the others, looking for us."

"And it might not. It might be those who burned the place out."

"I'll stay out of sight, until I'm sure."

"Leave the rifle."

Roan acted as if he didn't hear. "You rest, Tom."

"Roan!" he yelled at the boy as he passed out the rift in the wall. "Roan, leave the rifle!"

But Roan didn't answer.

He yelled again, "If you fire that rifle, shoot only one time."

Roan returned to the cave opening. "Why, Tom?"

"Hell, boy, any old backwoods poacher knows they'll not know where the shot came from if you fire only once. They'll be chasin' echoes."

Roan again turned to leave, and Tom called out one more time. "Be careful, son . . . and remember, McKeag riders don't back-shoot."

Roan carried the rifle low, running uphill away from the cave entrance until he reached a place where he could easily drop down and cross the creek, then up the willow-lined low embankment on the other side. The creek cut deeper and deeper into the mountain as it worked its way down the mountain. Roan knew a good spot, on the other side of the creek cut from where the cave was, a high spot, where he could look down on the trail and the coming riders, a spot backed up by a large stand of tamarack — eastern larch some called it. It was so thick a man could be ten feet from you and you'd never know it.

It was a quarter mile to the spot, but downhill most the way. The Hartford Sharps, with its tapered octagon barrel, was heavy, but the mission made it seem light to Roan. He trotted until he reached the tamarack, then went to the edge of a sharp cliff that fell away seventy-five yards down to the creek. He found a niche in the rocks, where he was well below the skyline, and where he could not only watch, but could rest the heavy-barreled rifle.

He waited.

And he didn't have to wait long.

Roan knew, and had liked, the man in the lead. It was the ramrod of the Bar X, Kelly Dugan. Roan was taken aback by this. He hadn't thought of the fact that Mr. Dugan might have anything to do with this. Roan had picnicked with the Dugans on the Fourth of July last year. He'd played with their little son, Kel.

He didn't want to shoot Kelly Dugan. But he was here, leading other Bar X riders across Lucky Seven ground. To Roan's surprise, they all dismounted at a spot where the creek pooled below a long run of white water, a spot they called Erin's Pool, as on warm summer days she used to come there to swim and bathe. Below the big pool, the water flowed much easier than the white water and pot holes above.

Roan had known it wasn't Dan when he saw them the first time. The big blood-red gelding was not among them, and Roan knew that horse and its smooth gait well.

There were four of them, and they led two pack mules. They began to make camp in a grass patch at the downstream side of the pool.

Curious, Roan laid the rifle aside and settled back to watch.

Three of them unsaddled, but Kelly Dugan did not. He helped them make camp, shook hands with the others, then mounted and started back down the mountain.

The remaining three erected a Goodyear rubber tent, set up a picket line for the horses and mules, then unpacked the panniers. Within an hour from the time they arrived, they'd set to work. One of them carried an ax and crosscut whipsaw, one a long whitewashed rod with marks in red up and down its length, and one a tripod with a telescope mounted on its top. The one with the ax and saw and the one with the rod wore large backpacks they'd taken from the panniers. They began at the pool, marking where the tripod man motioned after staring through the telescope, and reaching into their backpacks and retrieving and driving wood stakes. They yelled back and forth as they worked.

Roan was confused. If these were the same bunch who'd killed his aunt and friends, why were they messing about with tools and stakes?

He worked his way along the ridge above, watching them for over an hour. Confused and frustrated, he finally decided he hadn't run all this way for nothing — but he didn't want to kill the wrong men.

From over 150 yards away, he laid the rifle across the rim rock, folded away the long tang sight as it was a short-distance shot, and carefully sighted with the barrel-mounted buckhorn sight on the man carrying the ax and saw.

As Dan had taught him, he drew a bead, held his breath, released the first of the double set triggers, and slowly squeezed the second.

The booming report echoed across the canyon as the heavy .45-90 cartridge fired and bucked in his hands. The man spun, stakes and tools flying, and hit the ground. The other two dove for the brush.

Roan backed away, carrying the rifle in one hand, rubbing his shoulder with the other, and disappeared into the thick tamarack stand.

It took him an hour, carefully working his way through the tamaracks into the firs behind, always moving away from the cave, until he found a hard-rock face; then he turned north, up the creek canyon. He reached a point equal to where he had crossed the creek on the way down, and turned west down the canyon to the creek bottom, crossed the creek hopping from stone to stone, and up the other side, working his way carefully across rock where he could, until he reached the elder-berry bushes blocking the cave entrance. He'd checked his back trail a dozen times, but no one was dogging him. It would take a sharp-eyed Indian to track him.

Tom was sitting up, stirring a small pot

of something, when Roan entered. Roan crossed the cave, leaned the Sharps on the wall, then walked over and sat on a rock near the fire.

"Heard the shot," Tom said. "I guess it wasn't Dan?"

"Nope."

"So, what was the shootin' all about?"

"Tom, it was Kelly Dugan and three other fellas. They sat up camp at Erin's Pool . . . on Lucky Seven ground."

"What were they doin'?" Tom asked.

"I dunno. They had a thing on a tripod . . . a telescope . . . and they were walking out away from the creek, driving pieces of wood in the ground."

"Surveying."

"What for?"

"Laying out a road, or a ditch, or staking a claim. Who knows. So, what was the shot all about?"

"They was tresspassin'."

"They were trespassing."

"They were."

"So?"

"So, I shot one of them in his hind leg, if'n I hit him. I didn't back-shoot him, he was comin' face-on, Tom."

"You shouldn't be shootin' people if you don't know what they're about, boy."

Tom gave him a stern look.

"Well, I'll bet they ain't about it anymore. And they was about it on Lucky Seven ground. And they're with the bunch that shot Aunt Erin and Simon . . . at least they were with Kelly Dugan, and he's Bar X as sure as that mule of your'n dumps in the pasture."

"Aren't, not ain't. And were, not was." Tom, his side still paining him terribly, couldn't help but smile. "But I'll bet you're right. This trouble with the Bar X and Prager has come to a head in a terrible way. I knew Prager was a greedy old bastard, but I never thought. . . ."

"And I only shot one time."

"I heard that. That part, at least, is a good thing."

"So, who the hell was it?" Bert Prager swore at his ramrod.

"Bert, how the hell would I know? I was halfway down the mountain when I heard the shot."

Prager studied him for a moment; at least that's what Kelly Dugan thought he was doing. The fact was, he was wondering if he'd been lied to. *Had he paid for goods he hadn't received? There were only four graves he was sure of on the Lucky*

167

Seven. Badger Hotchkins had told him the others had been killed up on the mountain. So, who took a potshot at his newly hired surveyors? More than a potshot — with his leg blown all to hell, the man might never walk again.

Prager shrugged his shoulders and turned away. "Hell, get him into town and see what the doc can do." He turned back. "You don't suppose the Blackfeet are down this far, or the Shoshon? Any Indian sign about?"

"None that I've seen, and the boys haven't mentioned seeing any. Every track I've seen has been shod. Could have been rustlers, but why would they shoot at a survey party? Hell, where's the other McKeag hands and that nephew, Roan? Could have been anyone." Kelly was silent for a long moment, then added, "It could be if Roan and the rest of the hands are alive, they could be carryin' a real grudge."

"I don't know why," Prager snapped; then his tone eased. "Take the engineer into town and see if you can get the other two to head back up the mountain. Tell them we'll send a couple of guards along."

"Ha," Dugan said, "those two are headed back to Helena on the next Salisbury & Gilmer stage. Team of wild mustangs couldn't drag them back up that mountain."

"Then you gather up a couple of men and get back up there and find some sign. I want to know who did this. You can't shoot at Bar X men and get away with it."

Like you've had a couple of our men taking potshots at Lucky Seven riders? Dugan thought, but didn't say. Instead, he replied, "Thought you wanted me to take the surveyor to town to the doc's."

"Have somebody else do it. Hell, have him make his own damned way if you have to. Sounds like the others are headin' out anyways. I'll bet the beggars want to be paid. . . ."

Dugan sighed deeply. "I'll get up there this afternoon and see what I can find."

"Kelly, you take a couple of the boys with you. If there's shootin' going on, you want someone to watch your back. Is Jack Vance about?"

"He just got in from diggin' out the spring on the old Van Alt place."

"Take him. He's good with a gun — rumor is he's killed a half-dozen men in fair fights — and wouldn't back away from a gut-shot grizzly. Take Vance for the up close work, and take Shamus, he's as good with a long gun as we've got."

Chapter 14

Bert Prager sat on the porch awhile and considered this new development.

He wanted to mention to Kelly Dugan to watch out for the other dead riders from the Lucky Seven — so he could be satisfied they were dead — but the fact was he couldn't have known about them unless he was in on it, so he kept his mouth shut. It was long after Kelly, Shamus Pardee, and Jack Vance had ridden out when he pounded out the last of the pipe, spit the last bit of tobacco juice, grabbed up his crutch, and gimped his way back into the house.

He worked his way across the entry carpet, then heard voices coming from the kitchen. Who was in the house?

Careful to lay the crutch down on the polished spruce floors easily, he moved to the kitchen door. Elga, the housekeeper and cook, was talking with Meegan Dugan, Kelly's wife.

"So, what do you know about those four?" Meegan asked.

"You best drink yer tea, Mrs. Dugan. I don't repeat what I hear goes on in the house. Wouldn't be fittin'. These are fine apples for dried."

"Forget your pies for a minute. I don't like what I'm thinking, Elga. The McKeags were good folks, and now they're dead. And I can't go over there to see if there's anything I can do. Mr. Dugan won't have it — although he knows it's right."

"No reason to go — ain't nothing to be done. As I hear it, they're all dead and gone. You best mind what keeps you busy right here. God knows, there's plenty. Hand me that flour bin so I can get these pies started. I'll make an extra for you and the mister."

"So, did those four riders have anything to do with it? They were a hard bunch."

Bert Prager had heard enough. He crashed into the kitchen as best he could using the crutch. Meegan Dugan's face reddened as he snapped, "What the hell are you doing, woman, sticking your nose into Bar X affairs? You get on back to your little house — a house I might remind you provided by the Bar X — and tend to your own affairs."

Meegan glared at him, spun on her heel, and stomped out.

Elga kept her face down, working at the pie safe's tin shelf, making dough.

"Elga," Prager snapped, "you don't be listening into what doesn't concern you. If it's not sweepin' and dustin', it's not your affair."

She looked up with a wide smile. "And pie making. You like my pies, don't you, Mr. Prager?"

The hard look on Prager's face relaxed. "I like your pies just fine, Elga. And yes, the kitchen is your business as well."

"And you like the other wifely things I do for you?"

Prager reddened. "Don't get high-minded, Elga, or I'll send you packin' with nothing but the clothes on yer back."

She smiled, but Prager couldn't help but feel like it was a far too knowing smile, with the hint of she-wolf snarl lying beneath. Still, he gimped out to his office, and got to work on the books.

He would deal with Elga in his own good time.

One thing was for sure. He was going to have to have a talk with Dugan about his nosy wife.

Badger Hotchkins, Alvin Givens, Orin Slater, and Dutch Blodget made it to

Missoula, but Blodget was feverish — in fact, almost moribund. He still sat his horse, but barely. His eyes hadn't been open for the last twenty miles of the Mullan Road, and he'd been mumbling to his long-dead parents for most of that way.

The other three agreed that they had to get him to Missoula's fine hospital, but that could wait until the three of them washed the dust out of their craws. They reined up in front of the brick Headquarter's Building on Front Street, which housed the town's finest gambling establishment and saloon, better known to the more genteel as a "men's social club." Beyond it was a row of other less formidable buildings, saloons and whorehouses, referred to by the genteel as "sporting clubs."

Missoula, originally known as Hell Gate for the trading post that had been established there, lay on the Mullan Military Road, along the Hell Gate or Clark Fork River, its name depending upon who you asked. It was a thriving little town of five hundred. Of its twenty-five commercial buildings, almost half were saloons and "sporting houses." It was just the place for Hotchkins, Givens, and Slater.

Badger was surprised to see an old friend working the room, Shelaugh, the saloon girl who ran with Brownie and who had shot the McKeag fella down in the alley. Badger walked over and tapped the miner she talked to on the shoulder. "Take a walk, gent. She's mine for tonight."

"What —"

Badger laid his hand on the butt of his revolver. "Walk, I said."

The miner shrugged, and moved quickly away.

"Thought you was headin' out of the territory," Badger said, but he was smiling.

"Brownie and I took a liking to Front Street. Lots of suckers here."

"So, where's your old man?"

"He's laid up with the dyspepsia or poison bowel or some dang thing. I got him on the Prickly Ash Bitters. He'll shake it off in a couple a days."

"Good, then how about you and me —"

She backed away a step. She'd always feared Badger, and wasn't about to be alone with him. "I got the rot, Badger. You best take on one of the other girls."

"You'll go broke, woman. You better take up another trade."

She gave him a tight smile, then hurried off to tell the boss she was feeling poorly and was taking the night off. She didn't want to be in the same town as Badger,

Slater, and Givens, but she had no choice; she couldn't move on with Brownie laid up.

It was Orin Slater who, after three drinks, insisted they see Dutch on to the hospital. Missoula was already famous for the quality of its Sisters of Providence Hospital. Sisters' Hospital, as it was commonly known.

Badger glared at Slater, trying to figure which eye was looking at him, when he said they had to get Dutch Blodget over there before he died in the saddle.

"Bugger him," Badger said, and waved the bartender over to pour him another. "You take him, if'n you're so all-fired sanctimonious. I don't want to be within a mile of those papists. The women right here are more to my liking."

"You're a real genuine som'bitch, Badger."

Badger had killed men for less, but he was in too good a mood to get angry. He toasted Slater with his glass and a sardonic smile, then went back to talking to the round-faced buxom bar girl next to him.

"You coming, Al?" Slater asked Givens.

"Nope. I got a pocket full of money, and that wheel of fortune is calling my name." He subconsciously rubbed the scar on his cheek, which folded in a strange way when he smiled.

Givens' staying was fine with Slater. On the way out of town to the hospital, he stopped and dismounted well before they got there. He untied Dutch's bedroll from behind the wounded man's saddle, then tied it on the back of his own. Al Givens and Badger Hotchkins had forgotten — Dutch had 750 dollars cash money in that bedroll. Five hundred from the job for killing Dan McKeag, and 250 for cleaning out the Lucky Seven.

Slater had to carry Blodget inside. He flopped him down on the hallway floor just inside the door. Two sisters and a male attendant hurried over.

"He got his'sef shot in the leg, ladies." Slater reached in his pocket and generously handed the nearest sister a twenty-dollar gold piece. He winked his cocked eye. "He's a fair friend of mine, so take this as far as it goes."

One of the sisters, a wizened woman dressed in black with her head covered with a white-lined black hood, had already unwrapped the bandage on Blodget's leg. The putrid odor of flesh-gone-green filled the hallway.

The sister looked up at Slater, remorse

in her eyes. "It'll pay to have this limb removed, my son. We'll pray he lives. He's had such a portion blown out of this leg, we probably would have to remove it even if it wasn't rotten."

Slater headed for the door.

"Go with God," the sister called out behind him.

"Or the bloody devil," Slater said under his breath, low enough that he couldn't be heard.

He loped his horse, leading Blodget's, back to the Headquarter's. The horse would bring another 150 at least. Besides, he didn't want to miss out on the evening's festivities.

He'd already doubled his take from Old Man Prager, thanks to hardheaded Dutch Blodget; now he meant to double it again.

It was one of those nights where you felt you could reach up with your thumb and smear the layer of stars lining the night sky.

Pad reined up the phaeton at the edge of Deer Lodge. He'd convinced Dan that there was no hurry going to the Lucky Seven, and they'd passed right by the trail turnoff, as it might be occupied by those who'd burned the house down and killed

Erin and the others. And Dan was in no shape to seek revenge.

Dan had relented, as he was anxious to talk to only one man in the area, and that was Marshal Houston Greenlaw. Dan trusted Greenlaw. They'd hunted elk together on the Lucky Seven many times, their families had picnicked together and attended church together, and had Dan and Erin been blessed with a child, it was Greenlaw who Dan would have asked to be the baby's godfather.

But he didn't want anyone else to know he was alive, not yet, not until the strength came back to his right arm, or he became proficient with his left.

He lay low as they passed through town and out to Tin Cap Joe Creek, and finally reined up in front of the marshal's place. The two black-and-tan hounds met them with howls and barks, and Blue returned the favor. The dogs circled each other, growling and raising the hair on their backs, but finally settled into a tail-wagging truce.

Greenlaw was at the door, backlit by coal-oil lamps, by the time Paddy tied the traces to the brake handle and climbed down.

"It's Pad Dundee, Marshal Greenlaw."

"By God, you're a man who knows when

the pie's about to be served."

"I got folks with me. Can you step out here, please."

Greenlaw shaded his eyes and tried to peer into the night. Marshals had their enemies, but he had come to like Pad Dundee during their short time together, and besides, Pad was Dan McKeag's brother-in-law. He came on, without going back for his revolver.

Rose too had dismounted to stretch her legs. Pad introduced them, then said, "I've got a bit of a surprise for you, Marshal."

"Surprise or no, you can call me Houston. You too, ma'am."

Dan pulled himself up to a sitting position.

Greenlaw stared at him a moment, then shaded his eyes, gasped, and stared again. Only then did he speak. "By all that's holy, this is a surprise. You look pretty damn good for a fella's been dead a week or more, Dan."

"And you always did have a way with a compliment, Houston. I don't want anyone else to know I'm still kicking. Now, about that pie . . ."

With Pad on one side, Houston on the other, and Rose Ballard leading the way, they made their way into the house. Anne

Greenlaw dropped her spatula and turned white when she saw who they were helping to her kitchen chair.

Then after she collected herself, she ran over and hugged Dan.

"Careful, careful, Anne lass. I'm still sore as a boil."

"Sore is a dang sight better than what I was led to believe you were." She moved back at arm's length. "If you aren't a fine sight. Did you sit up in the casket, or what? I wouldn't put it past you."

"I take some killin', Anne."

"Well, as the Lord is my witness, I want to hear all about it, but while we're having this pie. I believe I got a good do on this one."

Rose helped her serve pie and coffee.

After they'd finished, Anne walked around the table to fetch Dan's plate. She bent and hugged him, whispering, "Dan, I'm so sorry about Erin."

"Thank you, Anne." He turned to Houston. "What do you know about what's happened?"

"Not much. Pad told you what we found at your place. I went straight over to see Prager. He played dumb. Did you sell out to him, Dan?"

"Like hell."

"He holds a deed. I made him show it to me."

"It's a fake."

"It carries your signature." Houston noted the look he was getting from Dan, and added, "At least it looks like your signature. And worse, it was witnessed by Judge Harley from Helena. Territorial Judge Harley."

"Oscar Pettibone Harley has gone to hell in a handbasket, Houston. He's a drunk and owes money to half the territory."

"That's true," Rose said. "He has a tab at my place that hasn't been paid in six months."

Pad too offered, "And he has a long string of notes at the bank. Even I knew about them."

Houston shrugged. "He's still a judge, and the most credible witness for a deed in the territory . . . if it comes to a court battle."

"To hell with the ranch," Dan snapped, "at least for a while. And court ain't the way this one's going to get settled. Right now, it's Prager and his hired guns I'm concerned with — and finding my nephew and unaccounted-for hands. And there's a little matter of a saloon girl name of Shelaugh."

"Honey," Houston called to Anne, who'd returned to the kitchen, "bring us some more of that sludge you call coffee." Then he turned back to Dan. "Four of Prager's 'hired hands' rode out of here, at least Prager said they did. And they were the ones claimed to have found the fire — and the bodies. I don't know anything about a saloon girl name of Shelaugh."

"And who were those four?" Dan asked.

"Al Givens is the only one I know of for sure."

"Rode out to where?"

"Denver, if you can believe Prager."

"Then it's probably Seattle. Did they associate with anyone else in Deer Lodge?" Dan asked.

"Not that I know of . . . wait . . . I remember that Al Givens visited some inmate at the penitentiary."

"Can you get over there tomorrow and find out what you can?" Dan asked, his look anxious.

"Damn sure can."

Anne returned with the coffee as Dan was saying, "We're going to find a camp spot up the creek."

"Over my dead body," Anne said. "I got a room here in the house for Rose. I know she could use some comfort after a night on the road. You two old hound dogs can sleep in the barn. There's a fine pile of new-mown meadow hay out there."

As Pad and Houston helped Dan out to the barn, Houston asked Dan straight out, "What do you plan to do, Dan?"

Dan's answer was low and deliberate. "Get well. Then, you don't want to know, Houston. You don't want to know."

"You should let the law take care of it, Dan."

"Judge Harley's the law."

"I knew you'd say that. You're going to put me in a bad position, my friend."

"Not as bad a position as Prager put Erin and Simon and Skeeter and whoever else is in those holes."

Marshal Houston Greenlaw didn't have an answer for that one.

Chapter 15

Rose got up with the sun.

No one else in the house was moving, so she put on a wrap over her nightgown and went to the kitchen, stoked up the fire and added a few sticks from the wood box, put on water for coffee, then walked out the back. Blue met her on the back porch with a wagging tail and cold nose.

To her great surprise, Dan McKeag stood outside the barn, his back to her. He was fully dressed, probably had slept in his clothes. He had one item added to his attire: Pad's left-handed holster. He was practicing drawing his revolver with his left hand. Drawing and aiming, time after time.

Barefooted, she crossed the yard, not speaking until she was only a few feet behind him. As she neared, she could hear him counting as he drew the weapon. He was up to seventy-eight. "You're up early," she said quietly.

Even so, she startled him and he flinched

before he turned. "Couldn't sleep. Haven't slept too well since I was shot up."

"But you're on your feet."

"I feel better. Not right yet by a long shot, but better. Soft hay and barn smells . . . and I slept better than I have been."

She moved away back toward the house, Blue pacing her. "I've got the coffee going, if you're interested."

"Be there in a minute. Got to practice a bit more."

It was only a few minutes before he appeared in the kitchen, moving slowly, but moving on his own. He took a seat at the table.

She served him. "You take cream?"

"Nope."

She sat also, eyeing him for a long time before she spoke. "You know I'm going to need to head back soon . . . tomorrow, in fact."

"I'm surprised you came along."

"I got attached to you while you were getting well."

He laughed. "Easy to do when a body's not talking back, not sassing you, and needing the attention. Women seem to attach to anything needs nurturing — even a sick ol' dog like me."

"Maybe, but I still don't want to see you

185

go off and get yourself killed. I'll have wasted all that time caring for you. Besides, you sassed plenty."

He turned serious. "I'll never forget what you did for me, Rose. You may have saved my life twice over, not only caring for me, but hiding me out like you did."

This time it was Rose who laughed. "No doubt about it, Dan McKeag. You owe me."

"How much?"

"You even try to pay me money and you'll be feeling real bad again, 'cause I'll black your eye."

He smiled and held up both hands as if to fend her off. "No offense."

"The devil you say. I am highly offended. I'm going to collect from you, but it's not going to be money."

"Then what?"

She looked at him a little coyly. "I'll have to give it some thought."

He shrugged.

She continued. "Dan, I don't want you to get yourself killed. Why don't you and Pad come back to Helena with me, and let Houston take care of things here."

Dan sipped his coffee and looked out the window before he spoke. "Rose, this is my problem . . . my life . . . and I've got to resolve it. I couldn't live with myself if I didn't. Besides, I still have no idea what's become of my nephew. I love that boy like a son. And I've got a ranch to get back from some low-down thief."

She stood and walked to the window, watching the sun rise, speaking without looking at him. "I know you have to finish this. You come see me when this is over."

"Yes, ma'am."

She turned to him. "You need to keep the phaeton and the team?"

"No, but I don't want you driving it all the way back by yourself. You take the Salisbury & Gilmer Stage . . . it's sixty dollars' fare, a newly refurbished Concord coach . . . real comfortable. I'll pay it . . . and I'll have Houston hire someone to drive your rig back."

She returned to her seat and reached across and covered his hand with hers. "You worry about getting well, and bringing all this to a safe and satisfactory conclusion. I'll get myself back and I'll arrange to have the wagon and team driven back. You've got enough to worry about."

"And I'll owe you?"

"Dang right, you'll owe me, and I expect you to stay whole so you can pay me back."

He smiled at her. "I promise."

★ ★ ★

Badger awoke with his mouth tasting like the stable muck pile; then he used his tongue to feel a cut on the inside of his lower lip. He raised a hand to the back of his head, feeling the knots there and a cut that was still seeping blood.

He shaded his eyes from the sun, peeking through the bars in the Missoula Jail window. He dropped his feet to the floor, then slowly stood. In the bunk across the cell he could just make out the ugly scarred features of Al Givens, and in the cell next to them, Orin Slater slept on the floor.

He moved a step and kicked the bunk where Givens snored. "What the hell got us in here?"

"Eh?" Givens managed to get his eyes open, rubbed them, then said, "What?"

"How'd we get in this hole?"

"You beat up a whore, and the coppers slipped up on us." Givens rubbed his forehead. "I got a knot here the size of a hen's egg from that sneak's damned bat."

"How come you and Slater are here?"

"We took umbrage at them trying to arrest you. Damn our stupid hides — we shoulda let you rot — and damn that whore anyways."

188

"Hey!" Badger yelled, hearing someone outside the cell. Then he walked to the bars. A jailer was moving down the hall. "Hey, when do I get out of here?"

"You clean up." He slipped a bowl of water and a towel under a four-inch passage where the door didn't meet the floor. "You got to see the judge this morning."

"What for?"

"Assault."

"And just who was I supposed to have assaulted?"

"Damn drunken sot. You broke Sally Sullivan's nose last night and closed both her eyes. You weren't nearly so tough when Paddget and Zigler invited you to come visit our little hotel here."

"She was . . . she was" — he thought fast, as he had absolutely no recollection of the event — "she was picking my pocket."

"If she was, she didn't do much of a job. You had several hundred in your pocket when we brought you in."

"I am getting it back?"

"Depends on what the judge says, friend. Like as not, you'll get some of it back. Clean up. You're first on the docket . . . 'cause you can afford to be." He laughed and Badger cringed.

As it turned out, there were no witnesses

to Badger's assault, only a badly beaten whore who had several prior arrests. Badger was fined one hundred dollars and given time served — one night — and Orin Slater and Al Givens fined twenty-five dollars each for disturbing the peace and interfering with an arrest. They were all on the street by lunchtime.

"Let's get the hell out of this piss-hole," Badger demanded as they entered the stable next to the jail. The hostler charged them another fifty cents apiece for the night's lodging of their horses, and when questioned, told Orin that his second horse — Blodget's — must still be tied outside the Headquarter's saloon. Before they left town, Slater rode back to the Headquarter's, fetched the horse, and sold it to the hostler for seventy-five dollars.

They joined back up at a café on Higgins Street, the town's main north-south street, across the alley from Missoula's largest building, the Missoula Mercantile.

"I'm going by to see how Blodget is getting on," Al Givens said, saddling up.

Badger shrugged, and turned to Slater. "Orin, I'm headin' to Flathead. I hear things is goin' good up there."

Slater shook his head in disgust. "You're piss-poor company, Badger, but I'm going with you. Money seems to favor you, and I favor it." The last thing Orin Slater wanted was to go see Dutch Blodget. The man might be in good enough shape to ask about his money, and Orin had gambled away all of Blodget's and most of his own. "I'm going with you nonetheless," Orin said, and mounted up.

"Stay out of them hotels with the bars in the windows," Badger said as they reined away from Givens.

Givens watched them ride away, then headed for the hospital, glad to finally be rid of the two of them.

When he reached the hospital, he found that Dutch's leg had been removed just below the knee, and that he would be there for a good while. If Orin Slater and Badger were heading north to Flathead, he decided he'd head south. He knew some fellas who used to hang out at Stevensville, near Fort Owen, a couple of days' ride south of Missoula on up the Bitterroot Valley, and decided this was as good a time as any to pay them a visit. Unlike the other two, he still had most of his money, and he intended to keep it.

Rose spent the day puttering about the house with Anne, who she came to like and admire. Anne was interested in Rose, and the fact she owned a saloon. To her, it was an aberration for a woman to be employed in any manner, particularly self-employed. She poked and prodded until she learned that Rose had inherited the place from her husband, who'd been killed by a stray shot while tending bar. He'd been gone more than three years, and Rose had made more of the place, doubling its size, since she was not burdened by his drinking up most the profits.

Pad found chores to keep him busy about the small ranch. He didn't look much like a ranch hand in his derby hat, but he'd been raised on a farm and fell right back into the regimen. He fixed fences, mended a couple of sad gates and stall doors, and worked on the water ditch.

Dan managed to spend some time repairing tack, and he saddled Dancer and rode to the end of Houston and Anne's eighty acres and back, but then he ran low on energy and, at Anne's insistence, ended up sitting on the front porch in the shade of the huge narrow-leaf cottonwood in the yard, scratching the heads of the two black-and-tans, to Blue's chagrin, and reading an Edgar Allen Poe book of poems

192

and stories. They only compounded his restlessness and dreary mood.

Just at dark, Houston rode into the yard. Pad took his horse, offering to rub it down and put it away in one of the newly repaired stalls. Houston made his way through the house directly to the porch where Dan sat, only pausing in the kitchen long enough to see what the women had conjured up for supper.

"What did you learn?" Dan asked as Houston stepped out, two glasses in hand, each with a touch of whiskey neat.

He handed one to Dan. "Seems Irish Bill Donagan is an old running mate of Al Givens, and knew one of the other boys as well. Irish Bill is in for murder — for life. The other one is a fella named Orin Slater, a cockeye'd tall slender fella. His eye doesn't impair his gun hand, howsoever. He's renowned as a fast gun with a dozen notches. Slater and Givens have a price on their heads down in Salt Lake. Seems they robbed a stage and killed the shotgun guard."

"How much reward? I might as well pocket some money. Wanted *dead* or alive, I hope?"

"Dead or alive — and it's two thousand apiece."

"Nothing on the other two?"

"He remembered something about one of them. The old boy's name was some animal. Buffalo, or Bison, or Wolf, or some damn thing . . . he couldn't remember exactly. By the way, you owe me an apple pie."

"Why's that?"

"Seems Irish Bill has a sweet tooth, and he wouldn't talk to me until I brought him an apple pie. I dabbled it out a piece at a time until I figured I knew all he did."

Houston laughed, but Dan was dead serious. "Any idea about where they headed?" Dan asked.

"Irish Bill didn't know. Givens only came by to see him one time. But he did mention another fella, Fat Anton Auchenbach. He and Givens served with Stonewall Jackson, and this Fat Anton has a trading post over Fort Owen way in the Bitterroot."

"That's it? Givens said nothing about Prager?"

"Irish Bill clammed up when I mentioned Prager's name. I got the feeling he might fear the old man. And Prager's bony hand can most likely reach beyond the place's stone walls."

"Many fear the old man. Then Fort Owen it is."

"I know the marshal over that way. I'll pen a letter for you."

"Thanks, Houston. What do I owe you for the pie?"

Houston laughed again, took a sip of his whiskey, then said, "My pleasure, Dan. I enjoyed the use of it, and took a piece for myself."

They sat in silence for a few moments, enjoying the warm evening.

Finally, Houston turned to Dan. "There's something I haven't told you yet, Dan."

"What's that?"

"There was another shooting up on the Lucky Seven."

"Who got shot?"

"Nobody you know. A surveyor. He was with a couple of other fellows, and with Kelly Dugan for a while, but Kelly wasn't there when the fella damn near got a leg blowed off."

"What happened?"

"Nobody really knows. They were surveying. Seems Prager is putting a ditch in, or wants to, up on Spotted Dog Creek. Shot came from up the mountain."

"Prager's not wasting any time getting his claws into the Seven. Did you check it out . . . I mean, who did it?"

"Nobody knows. Just a shot, from up the mountain."

"Tom, or Roan." Dan smiled broadly. "Damn if they're not alive, at least one of them."

"Maybe, but why shoot some poor stiff working for a living?"

"He was on the Lucky Seven, and they damn well know I wasn't planning a ditch. If Tom shot at the old boy and wanted him dead, it would have been between the eyes. He's as good as it gets with a Winchester."

"Don't think this was a Winchester. Too damn big a shell, maybe a Springfield .45-70 or a Sharps."

"Well, Tom carries a Winchester, and all Roan has is a LeMat I took off a Rebel officer, so maybe it was someone else."

"We can hope."

Dan laughed. "That it's Roan or Tom, or someone else?"

Houston merely shrugged.

Roan had ridden the paint down to Erin's Pool to make sure the surveyors hadn't returned. When he saw the camp vacant, he moved on down Spotted Dog Creek until he reached a spot at the edge of the firs up the mountain a half mile from the ranch buildings and what was left of the house.

He was not surprised to see three riders saddling their horses at the hitching rail outside the barn. He recognized one of the horses as they drew nearer. It was Kelly Dugan's gray. They were less than a quarter mile away when one of their horses must have smelled the paint, and whinnied loudly. Before Roan could cover the paint's muzzle, he answered.

The three riders reined up and stared in Roan's direction. He swung into the saddle and gigged the paint, who got his hindquarters under him and bolted into the stand of fir. Roan rode like a madman, boughs slapping at him, trying to knock him out of the saddle. He galloped for a quarter mile, then slowed to a lope, then a trot until he'd covered a mile or more. The hillsides falling away to the creek grew steeper and steeper as he moved up the mountain.

He found a game trail and let the paint pick its way up a rocky incline to a ledge a hundred feet over the creek bottom, then dismounted and studied the trail behind.

The three riders broke out of a copse of river willows lining the creek's bottom, less than a quarter mile beneath and behind him. He quickly dismounted and led the paint into the lodgepole pines behind him, tied the little horse where he couldn't be seen unless they topped the ledge, unscabbered the Hartford Sharps, and returned to the ledge.

The riders were three hundred yards behind — Dugan and one of the others had dismounted and were kneeling, studying his track.

They were for sure chasing him, and he for sure wasn't going to get caught by the likes of them.

Roan dropped to a prone position, hoisted the folding sight into its upright position, and rolled it to the three-hundred-yard mark. He cocked the big hammer, and sighted on the man still in the saddle — not Kelly Dugan — released the forward set trigger, took a deep breath, and squeezed.

Chapter 16

The boom reverberated down the canyon; Roan again was knocked backward. But not so badly this time, as he'd held the Sharps tight against his shoulder. The dun-colored horse the man rode went to its knees, and the man merely stepped off, then, looking surprised, dove into the willows.

I hit the horse, Roan thought, but didn't wait to study the situation more. He bolted into the trees, mounted, and set off at a steady hard clattering walk up the rocky hill, away from the men, away from the cave. Moving while his pursurers were still head-down in the brush.

Finally, it got so steep he had to dismount and lead the horse.

He hadn't traveled more than two hundred yards when a rock near his head splattered shards, stinging his face; then he heard the report of a rifle.

Far below he could hear Kelly Dugan yelling. "Don't shoot. He's only a boy."

Then Roan managed to lead the paint

behind an outcropping. He was out of sight and mounted, pushing the little paint hard. He spent all that day leading them away from the cave, if they followed. It was dark when he reached the rift, and entered.

Tom was on his feet, carving a couple of steaks from the doe's back strap.

"You been a long time," Tom said.

"Had some trouble."

"I heard the shot. More riders, or did you shoot us a fat elk? I hope it's the latter."

"Riders. Kelly Dugan again . . . and he saw me this time."

"Should we move outta this cave?"

"No, I led them all over the mountain afore I came back here. I don't even know for sure if they followed. I never saw them dogging my trail, at least after I let one go at them."

"Did you hit anything?"

"Damn sure hit a horse. He went to his knees, but don't know if I hit the damned Bar X rider."

"Watch your mouth. Erin would give you a slap."

"Anyway, I hit a horse."

It was late when Kelly Dugan, Shamus Pardee, and a very angry Jack Vance, riding double behind Pardee, plodded into the yard in front of Bert Prager's big Victorian house. Vance's tack was tied on behind Dugan's saddle. The light was burning in the sitting room Prager used for an office.

Prager limped out onto his porch in his nightshirt and yelled, "What?"

Kelly handed the reins of his gray to Pardee. "Rub him down good, Shamus." He then walked through the picket fence and up onto the porch. He smiled, but not so Old Man Prager could see. It was the old man's knotty knees below his night-shirt that amused Kelly.

"So . . . what?" Prager demanded.

"Didn't find nothing. Got shot at again. Shooter killed Vance's dun horse."

"He favored that horse. That one was his, not one of the string."

"He's mad as a hornet."

"So, who was it?"

"Dunno, Bert. Didn't get a look at him, or them."

Prager pulled at his beard and studied Kelly Dugan carefully. For some reason, the thought that Dugan was lying to him niggled him. He'd never had that feeling about Kelly Dugan before. "You sure?"

Kelly's amusement was long gone, and

he raised his voice. "Damn sure. I said I didn't, and I didn't."

"Get some sleep."

Kelly stomped off.

The next morning, Prager was having coffee in the bunkhouse kitchen when the men came in. He seldom met with the men in the bunkhouse, preferring to awe them with the big house when he gave orders to his hands, which he seldom did as he normally let Kelly Dugan take on that task. Now that the four hired shooters were gone, he was down to eighteen hands.

He jawed with them until they'd finished eating beans and biscuits laced with honey, then turned to Jack Vance. "Vance, come on up to the main house before you saddle up."

"Yep," Vance said, then followed the old man as he limped along to his porch. He seated himself in the rocker, and yelled to Elga for coffee for the two of them. Vance was a tall angular-faced man with a shock of black hair that normally hung over his forehead. His hawk nose had been broken more than once and the bridge was a crooked track, and his heavy-boned hands were scarred on every knuckle.

"Heard you lost that dun horse?" Prager asked, stroking his black beard.

"I did. I'll never replace that horse. He was game for anything and moved like a freight train."

"Dugan gave me some cock-and-bull story last night. You want to tell me what really happened?"

"We were a half mile or so up the mountain from the McKeag place —"

"It's the Bar X now."

"A half mile up the mountain, following the track of what Dugan had thought he'd seen, and sure enough, there was the track of a single rider. Anyway . . ."

Elga exited the house and handed them both a cup of coffee.

Vance continued. "Dugan and Shamus had dismounted to study the track, and by God if the shooter didn't blow my dun horse right out from under me. Horse went to his fore-knees, down like a dropped anvil, then rolled over dead as a stone."

"And the shooter?"

"I mounted Shamus's piebald, and Dugan and I set off after the dirty craven dog what shot my dun. We came to where we could see him heading up the mountain way up ahead. I jumped off the piebald and layed down on him at four hundred yards, and pulled off."

"And?"

"And Dugan went nuts. Hell, the young fella had shot at us, and I meant to kill him. First shot was just for distance, I'd' a hit him with the second, but I never got it off."

"Young fella?"

"Yeah, Dugan was yelling, 'He's just a boy. Just a boy.' He knocked my rifle aside afore I could get my kill shot off, then he wouldn't give chase and made me hold off. I truly wanted to kill him dead."

Prager nodded his head a few times, then changed the subject. "You're a fair hand with cattle, Vance, and a fine hand with that revolver. I hear that you draw, somebody smells the smokes of hell. To be truthful, that's why you got hired on. I got some special work for you, and it sounds like you might just like the job. And if Kelly Dugan keeps doggin' it, there might just be a far better job available. You harbor any compunction 'bout killing men?"

Elga came out with the coffeepot, and topped off their cups. Prager remained silent until she went back in the house. Then he turned back to Vance. "You interested in doing some manhunting?"

"If it's that whelp what shot my dun, and if the pay's healthy, I'm damned interested."

★ ★ ★

The following morning, Dan said good-
bye to Rose in front of Houston's house.
She wore a traveling suit with full skirt and
a crisp white blouse. Her eyes were bright
and skin pale, with a touch of red on the
cheeks and more on the lips. Pad was to
drive her into Deer Lodge to catch the
stage.

"Am I ever going to see you again?" she
asked, standing less than an arm's length
from him.

"I hope so, Rose. I can't think about —"

"I know you can't, Dan. It's too soon. I
wouldn't think well of you if you did. It
wouldn't be seemly. But mourning doesn't
take a year as some fools think proper, and
I'll bet your wife . . . Erin . . . I'll bet she
wouldn't want you to mope about for a
year." She gave him a devastating smile.
"I'll see you back in Helena when and if
you're ready to come."

She stepped forward and bussed his
cheek with hers.

Dan felt a small catch in his throat. She
was a fine woman, felt fine, and smelled
even better. He would go to Helena when
and if he would consider things like that
again. And he would look Rose Ballard up.

Pad had given them some time, but now

he exited the house, carrying her valise. "Why, Miss Ballard, yer as pretty as a new heifer in a flowerbed."

"Why, thank you, Pad, I think."

They both laughed, then Pad added, "They don't hold those stages for no one, even fine-lookin' ladies." He escorted her to the phaeton and helped her up. Dan stood watching. He tipped his hat as Pad whipped up the buggy. She continued to watch him, and he her, until they disappeared into a grove of cottonwood. Blue trotted along behind them until they reached the copse of trees, then hesitated, looking back and forth at the phaeton and the porch. Finally, he turned and trotted back to where Dan had taken a seat in the rocker. He whined for a moment, until Dan silenced him. "I know, boy, I'm going to miss her some too."

"We'll all miss her. That's a fine woman . . . a fine lady," said Anne, who had walked up behind him.

Dan was silent a moment before he looked up at Anne. "She said for me to come to Helena, should I have the urge."

"You will. She cares a lot for you, Dan McKeag. If you go, you'll be twice blessed, and Erin would want you to be."

Dan turned to face her. "Erin said that?"

Anne laughed. "Dan, women talk about a lot of things while they're messin' about doing for you men. Erin and I jabbered a lot, and not all of it was about how worthless you menfolk are. I loved her as I love you; as Houston and I do. We talked of what might happen should you men meet your maker while we're still young, and of what we'd like to happen should she or I go long before either of you. We both agreed that we'd like our men to go on and be happy . . . with a fine lady. It wasn't something either of us wanted to dwell on, but it was spoken of."

"And you think Rose —"

"I know, she runs a saloon, and works as hard as any man. She was a victim of circumstance. I'd like to think I'd have done as well as she's done, given the circumstance. I wish you'd go with her right now, and forget Prager and the others. The Good Lord will shuttle him off to hell when he has that decision to make."

"She said it wouldn't be seemly, and it wouldn't. I got to let my feelin's settle. And right now, my heart's as cold as a glacier in the high country." Dan smiled, but it wasn't a kind one, it was tight-lipped. "I'm going to hurry Prager on his way when the time comes. But first, I've got to find

Roan. Then I want the men who watched her die and the woman who shot me down like she was killing a hog to butcher. Less remorse maybe . . ."

"Vengeance is mine, sayeth the Lord," she said quietly.

He stared off to the west. "Not this time, Anne. Not this time. The Good Lord is going to have to take second fiddle this time, and as He is my witness, I don't think He's going to mind a bit. In fact, I imagine He's encouraging the devil to stoke the fires of perdition."

Anne walked back into the house and left Dan to his thoughts. She paused at the door and glanced back.

He was again practicing drawing and aiming the Remington revolver.

Blue whined a plaintive sound, chased his tail in a circle, then settled on the porch.

"Tom, I had me a dream last night."

"Dreams can be good things, boy."

"This one wasn't."

"How so?"

"Either she was here in this cave, or I dreamed that Erin came to me."

Tom sipped the last of the coffee they had. "I hope she was telling you to go find

Dan, and forget about keeping those fool Bar X riders off the Lucky Seven."

"Just the opposite. She was yelling at me, wondering why I hadn't shot 'em all down yet." Roan's face reddened. "Tom, she ripped open her blouse and I could see right through the holes in her chest."

"That wasn't no dream, son, that was a nightmare. It'll pass soon enough and you'll be sleeping like that ol' log we be usin' for a bench outside."

But Roan didn't return Tom's smile. "She was speakin' to me from the grave, Tom."

"The hell you say. It was that tough old whitetail rump steak we gnawed on last night. You had the stomach epizootics is all. Go out there and shoot us a tender elk, and we'll fill our bellies and both sleep better."

"I will. I saw a herd over in the aspens last night. But . . . she was speakin' to me. Erin . . . from the grave, Tom."

"That's fool talk, Roan. I'm takin' good deep breaths finally and gonna be mended enough to ride here soon, and we're gonna circle around and get to town — and we'll go see Marshal Greenlaw. Maybe he knows where Dan is, and maybe he'll listen to you about those fellas shot Erin and Simon and burned the place down."

"She came to me, Tom. In the night."

"Go kill us an elk, boy. Keep yourself busy, leave the law to do its duty, and don't think no more about Erin or the Bar X riders. We'll skirt around, and go to town. Maybe tomorrow."

Chapter 17

Pad had convinced Dan that they should not set out to find Roan, then for Fort Owens, for at least two more days, until Dan could heal some more, and until Pad could ride one of Houston's nags into town and buy himself a decent horse. Fort Owens was at least 150 miles from Houston's place, and there was no telling where they were heading after that.

Dan agreed because he still wanted to have Houston nose around town and see what he might learn about where Roan might be — if the boy was alive, someone must have heard something. The best he could figure from the description Houston had given him of the men in the graves, it was Simon Coppersmith, Poker Pete, and Skeeter. That meant Roan, Tennessee Tom, and Slim John were still out there somewhere.

He had to at least find Roan before he rode off to avenge Erin. And Simon. And Skeeter. And Pete. No telling who else. And avenge himself.

Jack Vance cut a tall sorrel out of the remuda and double-blanketed him before fitting his saddle. He planned to ride hard and long if necessary, and didn't want the animal to go sore-backed on him.

He borrowed a shiny new 73 Winchester from Prager, and left his own beat-up Springfield trapdoor in the bunkhouse. A box of .44-40 shells would fit both the Winchester and his Colt. Prager had offered him five hundred dollars a head for any of the remaining three Lucky Seven hands, including the boy.

It was potentially more money than Vance had earned in a half-dozen stage and trail robberies when he was a younger man in California. He'd thought that kind of life was long behind him, and that he was getting a little long in the tooth, but this was just too much money to turn down. One thing was for sure, he was still a fast gun, and he hit what he drew down on. Some might have a qualm about killing a boy, but Jack Vance had ridden with Bloody Bill Anderson — William Anderson was one of Quantrill's Raiders, one of the most heinous, and Vance had been one of the seventy who'd ravaged and pillaged Centralia, Kansas — he'd killed women and children before. His place in hell was already reserved, and he knew it.

It was mid-morning when Vance got to the Lucky Seven ranch buildings. He made a small camp in the barn and cooked coffee and warmed some biscuits, and it was almost noon by the time he worked his way up to the spot where he spooked some crows and a couple of turkey vultures — his horse stared vacantly, its big sad eyes picked out. It made him angry all over again. He headed up to where he'd seen the boy take off up the steep escarpment of shale, topped it, and began a methodical search for sign.

He stopped short and snapped up his head as a shot reverberated down the canyon, then a half minute later, another followed. The second he was able to zero in on. He determined that it came from the other side of the creek, a mile, maybe more, high up in the timber.

He remounted the sorrel and gigged him into a steady but swift walk, back down to the bottom and across the creek, and up the heavily timbered west side.

He could feel his purse growing fatter with every hoofbeat.

It took him more than an hour to climb to where he thought the shots had come from. It was a thickly wooded mountain-side.

He found a small spring high up among some firs, a grassy spot that was good for the horse. It would make a good camp. He unloaded his bedroll and hoisted his grub sack up high in a fir using his reata. Then he began a methodical search of the mountainside. It would take the rest of the afternoon unless he was particularly lucky.

But he was a patient man. He'd hunted men before, and knew patience was a good part of the process.

Dan walked out to the barn, where Paddy was working on some saddle trees and tidying up Houston's tack area in the barn. Houston was a fine marshal, but not much of a rancher.

After working on a saddle for a while, repairing some leather ties and sewing up a torn saddle fender and busted traces, Dan began to tire.

"If you want to get your butt back in the saddle, you go rest," Paddy insisted. "You need to sharpen your horns a bit more before we go on the prod."

Dan shrugged, but relented. He walked through the house, bummed another cup of coffee from Anne, and carried a copy of the weekly *Deer Lodge Tribune* out to the front porch and the rocker.

Angered, he saw where the sale of the Lucky Seven and most of McKeag's Mountain to Bertoldus Prager of the Bar X was announced. There was also an article reporting his demise in Helena, and the untimely fire at the Lucky Seven, where four poor souls, including Dan McKeag's wife, newly widowed, lost their lives.

The demise of the McKeags, a respected family, was mourned, and the article was bordered with a thick black line. It was reported that it was all a terrible circumstance that would go down as one of the saddest weeks in Deer Lodge City history.

He let the anger find and settle in a place deep in his center, then went on to other news. He was engrossed in an article describing over ten thousand deaths in the Southern states from yellow fever when a low growl from Blue made him look up.

As engrossed in the article as he was, he hadn't heard the young man who stood at the gate, staring at him.

"Grant, how are you?" Dan asked. It was the young man from the telegraph office in Deer Lodge, Grant Hodges.

"Mr. M-M-McKeag," the young fellow

stuttered, white in the face, looking like a rabbit in a wolf's mouth.

"It's me, Grant. No matter what you might have heard, I'm alive and pretty well."

"I . . . I have a wire for . . . for Marshal Greenlaw. He wasn't in his office, and I thought . . . I thought he might be here."

Dan couldn't help but laugh aloud. The young man stood at the gate as if he was about to bolt. "Well, Grant, if you'll stop stuttering like a man with new store-bought teeth, you can bring it on in."

When he reached the step, Dan rose and extended his hand. "How you been?"

Hodges hesitated, but finally took the hand, then seemed surprised that he actually caught hold of it. "I'm fi . . . fine, sir. We all . . . all heard you were shot and buried."

"Sit down, Grant. I need to talk to you about that."

Grant leaned against the porch rail, still looking as if he might break and run, saying nothing, as Dan retook the rocker. Blue moved up on the porch to lay beside him, but kept his eyes on the young telegraph operator.

"A couple of weeks ago, my brother-in-law, Paddy Dundee, sent Mrs. McKeag a telegram, asking her to come to Helena," Dan said.

"Yes, sir. I remember that."

"What happened to that telegram?"

"Sir?"

"What happened? Did you deliver it out to the ranch, or pay someone to do so, or what?"

The man reddened. "I don't remember."

Dan could see he was lying, and lying rather badly.

"Now, Grant, you've known me for a long time, right?"

"Yes, sir."

"And you know I'm not a man to condone lying."

Grant reddened even more.

"And if a man lies to me, he's liable to get himself in a very bad way." Dan slipped the Remington from its holster and spun the cylinder, checking the loads, eyeing the big gun. Then he looked back up at Grant Hodges and centered icy blue eyes on him. "A very, very bad way. And after I put him in a bad way, if there's anything left of him, I'd turn him over to Marshal Greenlaw, who, as you well know, is a man who doesn't mind taking the thirteen turns in a hemp rope."

"It . . . it . . . it was Mr. Prager, sir."

"Mr. Prager what?"

"He pays me."

"For what, Grant?"

"He gets a look at any telegrams that come in related to the cow business, or mining, or just about anything."

"Pays you how much?"

"Five dollars a month. Cash money."

"And does Western Union know anything about this?"

This time Hodges didn't redden, but rather turned white. "No . . . no, sir. My boss in Helena, he'd probably fire me. Telegrams are supposed to be private . . . to the addressee only. Mr. Prager took it. Said he was heading out that way and would deliver it to Mrs. McKeag for me. It's a long ride out there."

"That's what I thought. So, Grant, what do you think I should do? You know Mrs. McKeag and some others got killed out on the Lucky Seven?"

"I heard that, sir. A big fire, I understand."

"Some low-down murdering scum killed them, Grant. They were all murdered, my dear wife included, and your not delivering that telegram to the . . . to the *addressee,* I believe you said . . . well, that may have been a contributing factor to my wife being murdered. In fact, you could be an accessory, and a candidate for that hemp rope and hellfire."

"My God," Grant muttered. Dan thought the young man was going to have apoplexy and pass out right there.

"Grant, I don't want anybody to know I'm out here and alive. Do you understand?"

"Yes, sir. Anything, Mr. McKeag. Far as I'm concerned, you're cold meat."

"I mean no one. Not even your sainted mother, not your woman, if you have one. Don't even talk about it to Jesus. Understand?"

"I understand, sir."

"Now, give me that wire for Mr. Greenlaw, and I'll see he gets it."

Grant straightened, suddenly righteous. "I'm not supposed to give this to anyone other than the addressee."

"Grant, you're making me angry."

"Yes, sir." He handed over the telegram, nodded, and moved quickly out to the gate and his horse.

"No one, not for a month, or more, not till I tell you it's all right, you understand?" Dan called after him.

"You got my word of honor, sir."

For whatever that's worth, Dan thought, but didn't say.

Hodges mounted and gigged the old horse into a trot.

Anne walked out of the house. "Who was that, Dan?"

"Grant Hodges, from the telegraph office."

"Did he see you?"

"Yep, but I think we settled it. In fact, I think he'll go to the grave with it."

She looked worried for a moment, then nodded at the onionskin envelope. "That for us?"

"It's for Houston."

She reached out and took it. "Why don't you have Paddy kill us a chicken or two. Could you stand a little fried chicken?"

"Yes, ma'am. In fact, I'll kill a couple and pluck 'em myself. We're riding out in the morning, and it'll be our last home-cooked meal for a long while, I imagine."

"Too soon, Dan. You sure you're ready?" She tucked away a strand of gray hair into her dust cap.

"Nope, not sure, but I'm going anyway. Should that young fella flap his pie-hole, it could bring trouble out here to you folks, and I don't want that."

"Pshaw. Houston and I've seen trouble before, and we'll see it again. Trouble follows Houston like a bull elk on a hot cow — pardon the expression. It comes with the badge."

"Not because of me, it doesn't. We're leaving at first light."

"You talk that over with Houston when he gets home."

Dan smiled and nodded, but no one could convince him not to go. He called after her, "Don't let the shooting bother you, Anne. It's just me blowing up some peach tins . . . and some steam off."

She shook her head and sighed. "I've heard gunfire before, Danny," she said, her tone a little exasperated. Then she went back to her kitchen.

Dan went to set the empty tins on the fence rail out behind the barn.

It was time.

He shot up a full box of shells, quick-drawing left-handed, still not able to hold firm with his right, and to his surprise hit most of what he shot at — his hours of practice had paid off. Paddy and Houston came riding up to the barn, Paddy leading one of Houston's old nags and riding a fine tall black gelding horse with white feet and a white blaze on his nose.

"Sounds like Gettysberg and the damn war," Houston said.

Pad smiled his crooked grin, and gave

the new gelding a look. "I'll be forking one that'll give Dancer a run for his money," he said, dismounting and handing Dan the reins. "You want to ride some good horse-flesh?"

"I'll take your word, Pad. But it's a good thing if he's fast and tough. In the morning, we're going to test him. We're riding by the ranch to say our good-byes to Erin, and God willing, we're gonna find Roan. Then we're gonna to take some heads."

"I'm going in the house," Houston said. "I don't want to hear this kind of talk." He walked off.

"In fact," Dan said, with a tight smile, "we're gonna take some heads right now."

"Eh?" Paddy said, giving him a funny look.

"Chicken heads. Anne wants a couple of chickens to fry up for dinner."

"Good, I do love me fried chicken. And I'm hungry as the woodpecker who worked on the whiskey barrel and has a hangover headache." They headed for the chicken pen. Paddy reached the door first, but didn't enter. Rather, he turned back to Dan. "You sure you're up to this? There's a bunch of bad old boys out there."

"Paddy, they don't know I'm coming,

and I'm not gonna give 'em any more warning than they gave me in Helena, or gave Erin, Simon, Pete, and Skeeter."

Paddy shrugged and entered the henhouse. But Dan continued talking.

"Pad, I haven't said much to you about all this. I really don't expect you to go along —"

Paddy spun to face Dan, looking up into the taller man's face. All humor was gone from Pad. He spoke slowly and deliberately. "Erin was me little sis, Dan McKeag. I'm going after them old boys, if'n or not you come along. If you die, then I'll finish it, and if I catch it and die on you, I expect you to do the same. The only thing that's gonna stop us is waking up with candles around the bed. I'm going to rip off some heads and piss down their neck-hole." Then he smiled that crooked smile. "It's going to be a real jollification, far as I'm concerned."

"Then that settles it. By the way, what did you name that big black you bought?"

"His name was Angel, but now it's Lucifer. He's hot as a two-dollar French whore — and on the trail of some nonrepentant sinners. Figured it suited our little mission, and his, a lot better."

Dan sighed deeply. "Could just."

223

Chapter 18

While the Greenlaws, Paddy, and Dan were enjoying fried chicken, mashed potatoes, gravy, greens, and biscuits, Kelly and Meegan Dugan were having a peacemaking hug after a long argument.

She pushed him away and stood looking up at him, his cheeks cradled in both her soft hands. "Then it's settled, Kel," she said. "It'll be best for little Kel, that's a sure thing."

"It is. And you're right. Start packing." He spun on his heel, left their little house, and walked straight to the big house.

He rapped on the door, and Elga came and opened it for him. "He's in his study, his nose in a pile of papers," she said, drying her hands on a kitchen towel. "You want I should bring you something to drink?"

"No, ma'am, I don't expect I'll be long."

Prager looked up when he walked in. "What?"

"We're packing up, Bert."

"What. You going somewhere?"

"I'm drawing my pay."

Kelly expected an argument. Prager had always said that Kelly was the best cattleman he knew, next to himself, and he was surprised when Bert bent, reached under the desk, and fished out his little strongbox. He opened it, checked the calendar on his desk, and counted out what Dugan had coming.

He handed the gold coins over, and snapped, "You do fine with cattle, Dugan, but you just don't have the stomach for the hard part of staying alive in a hard country."

There were a lot of things Kelly could have said to Bert Prager, but he didn't. He merely extended his hand. "I appreciate all these years of employment, Bert. I'm taking Meegan and little Kel to town —"

"With the rest of the lily-livered."

Kelly was beginning to redden, but he merely spun on his heel and left.

It was a fine morning to begin.

They avoided Deer Lodge City, and it was noon before they got to the ranch.

They sat in the pines overlooking the Lucky Seven for several minutes, studying the ranch buildings below, making sure no one was about. Blue busied himself making sure a squirrel didn't get down out of his tree. Dan hushed him when he barked. He looked properly chagrined, and came back to stand by Dancer.

It was hard for Dan to even look at the place, with the home he and Erin had worked so hard to build nothing but a pile of burnt timber.

While Pad went to the barn to make double sure no one was about, Dan and Blue poked through the charred pile that had been home for so many years. He avoided even looking up the hill at the grave sites.

Every burnt and twisted item seemed to bring back a memory.

Pad returned. "Dan, there was somebody camping in the barn last night, or the night before. Campfire in the middle of the barn floor still has embers."

"I'll take a look in a while, but first, let's go say our good-byes. It's been far too long."

They stood for a long while at the gravesides, hats in hands, heads bowed, neither saying a word. Blue lay with his nose between his forepaws, whining softly.

Finally, Dan looked up, his face streaked with tears. "I wish I had the words."

"It don't take words, Danny boy. What you feel in your heart is all that counts."

Dan settled his broad-brimmed hat on his head, spun on his heel, and headed for the barn. He didn't say it to Pad, but at the moment, his heart felt like a block of ice, and his blood ran cold, as if full of shards.

He walked about for a long while, studying sign, both inside and outside the barn.

Several of the horses from his string were still pastured in the fenced forty at the barn's side, but he saw little untoward, except for what he presumed were bloodstains on the tack room floor. The forty-acre horse pasture was fed by a small spade-dug offshoot of Spotted Dog Creek. It was June-deep in grass, and the animals could stay there another month unattended.

Finally, Dan walked out to Dancer and mounted. "Last man here left off up the mountain. Left rear shoe has a bad nick in it. Tall horse, long strides, he won't be hard to track."

"Why track him? Probably one of the Bar X riders," Paddy answered as he swung up into the saddle.

"We're going up the mountain anyway. We'll follow him a while, just for general principles. If his animal carries a Bar X brand, maybe we'll brand his naked backside and send him home afoot."

It was a fine fat young elk cow. Roan had shot her high on the mountain. Not dropping her with the first shot, he'd taken a second, and she'd folded on her front legs and was dead by the time he reached her.

It had taken him a couple of hours to gut her, strip away her back straps and one hindquarter, and load the little paint. He'd never had the paint around a new-shot elk, and the little horse had been skittish. It had taken Roan another half hour to calm him down and get him loaded.

Then he'd cut away the remaining hindquarter and forequarters, moved a hundred yards from the kill site as Dan had taught him, and hoisted them high in a fir tree with his lariat to keep the bears off the best part of the meat.

He and Tom had feasted on a thick chunk of back strap that night. Tom had chastised him for taking the second shot, but he'd assured Tom he'd waited a long while, sitting on a high ridge, studying the mountain below, making sure no one came up any of the trails he could see.

Still, Tom worried.

Now, in first light of morning, Roan was on his way back to fetch the other quarters.

Tom was ready to try the saddle, so they'd be leaving soon to go down the mountain and try to find Marshal Greenlaw, but just in case, it would do to have the cave well provisioned. Just in case.

It would be a fine sunny day, but this early, there was a heavy mist on the mountain. It was quiet walking, and even the little horse made no noise.

Roan was not surprised, when he arrived where he'd gutted the elk, to see he had some competition. He'd had to force the paint, single-footing, the last quarter mile to his destination. The animal's ears were forward, his nostrils flared, his eyes ringed with white, and he spooked like he'd been jabbed with a hot poker at every cone that fell from squirrels cutting their winter stash. Roan rode the last of the way with the Sharps resting across his saddle.

And, as Roan had been taught to trust, the paint, with his far superior nose and ears, was a fine indicator of danger.

A fat cinnamon grizzly sow and two yearling cubs, one blond and one black, were head-down in the gut pile. Mama might have gone five hundred pounds, and the cubs were near one hundred. Seven hundred pounds of pure mean was a whole lot more than the boy was prepared to face.

Roan cussed himself for leaving the heart and liver, then reined up over 150 yards away, but even that, he knew, was not a safe distance. A full-grown griz could cover a hundred yards far faster than the paint could; in a four-count, Dan had told him. Luckily, the only time he'd seen a griz run, it was running away up a steep mountainside, but he knew to respect their speed and power.

He dismounted. The fir with the quarters high in its branches was on a level with the bears, but off to the right. The wind was in his favor, but even as busy as the bears were, he didn't think he could get to the meat stash without attracting their attention . . . and he sure didn't want to be four seconds from them. A glance away, and teeth and claws could be on him before he glanced back.

He could wait, or he could fire over their heads and try to scare them off. What to do? Tom seemed in a hurry to get down the mountain, now that he thought he could ride. Roan could also abandon the meat. But what a waste.

From experience, Roan knew even a griz

would normally run for the hills with the scent and sight of man, but he also knew they'd protect a kill, or a food source, and particularly protect their young against any threat.

He would have to think this through. He remounted and, much to the pleasure of the trembling paint, backtracked a hundred yards up the mountain to where he could sit on a rock, watch the bears feed, and study the situation.

Thanks to a half-dozen crows and magpies, Jack Vance had found the elk kill the night before — luckily for Roan, just after the boy had ridden away, and just as the sun was dropping behind the mountain.

He saw that there was a single hunter, and tracked him long enough to see that he'd stashed the quarters up the fir tree. He dropped the meat down, carved himself off a generous slab of hind-quarter, and hoisted it back up the tree. He knew the hunter was returning, and also knew it would be difficult or impossible to track him in the failing light. Why do so? All he had to do was wait.

He'd be back in the morning, Vance surmised, and Vance would be waiting.

The hunter would become the hunted.

And he had done so, arriving at the kill

site just after dawn, his belly full from roasted elk rump both from a late supper and an early predawn breakfast.

He'd found a spot well up the mountain where he could watch the kill from a distance, and with full light and sighting the grizzly threesome feeding on the gut pile, he was happy he had. It wouldn't do to stumble on the three griz while they were enjoying the feast the hunter had left them.

And he'd seen the man on the paint horse approach; the boy, he surmised, as it was the same paint that had scrambled up the steep escarpment, allowing Jack to get off a shot when he was with Kelly Dugan and Shamus. He was glad he'd missed, because now his target was worth five hundred dollars to him.

Of course, the boy might be camping with the other two, the black former ramrod of the Lucky Seven and the one they called Slim John. If they were still alive, if Badger Hotchkins had lied about all the others being killed, as well as the boy. And Jack Vance figured Badger Hotchkins would lie even when the truth would serve him better.

Jack decided it would be much tougher to find the others if he shot the boy down, so he would wait, and follow, and let the boy lead him back to the others. He could be looking at fifteen hundred, if all three of them were there for the taking.

He smiled to himself, watching the boy on the rock across the canyon, knowing that he was waiting for the griz to either finish or bury what was left of the gut pile, so he could retrieve the meat.

Jack was in no hurry.

Dan led, carefully studying the trail before him, after cautioning Pad to keep an eye out for anyone ahead, or a bushwacker in the rocks. It was a long, tedious process, but they finally came to where their quarry had seemed to be headed one way, then had backtracked at a trot, and occasionally a gallop where terrain allowed. It was two hours before they came upon the remains of a camp high on the mountain, beside a small spring. A pair of crows flew out of the camp ahead of them. Several trails came and went, but after careful study, Dan found the trail he believed was the last time the horse with the nicked shoe left. It headed out east, back toward Spotted Dog Creek Canyon.

Finally, the old sow and her cubs got their fill and left the gut pile, now nothing but stains on the forest floor. One of the cubs dragged the pelt away with them. Normally, Roan would have kept the pelt, but he knew he wouldn't be at the cave anywhere near long enough to prepare it for tanning, and it was too heavy to haul with them.

Roan gave the three griz plenty of time to get away, then went down and lowered and packed the remaining three quarters on the still-nervous paint. He'd have to walk himself, as the little paint couldn't carry him and the load.

He tied together the forequarters and draped them across the forks, taking a turn around the horn. He was positioning the hindquarter on the cantle, trying to make it ride level, when he noticed a clean cut where a three-pound chunk of meat had been removed.

Stopping stone-cold in his movements, Roan contemplated what that meant. He searched his memory, questioning what was before his eyes. No, he hadn't cut anything from the hindquarter. But sure as God made this forest, a chunk of meat was cleanly taken. The only thing that could have gotten to it would have been a bird, or a small animal who could climb, and there were no claw or beak marks, only a clean cut. He slipped the LeMat from its holster and studied the forest across the back of the paint, acting as if he was still concentrating on tying the load. Then he ducked under the horse's neck and, using the horse for cover, did the same, studying the forest behind.

Damn, what was going on here? He felt a chill down his spine as if something, or someone, was watching from the shadows of the deep fir forest. Was the bear back . . . but no, the bear hadn't taken a clean slice from a hindquarter twenty feet up a fir. He knew enough about the griz to know they didn't climb trees like a black bear could. It had to be something, no, someone else.

There was nothing to do but move on, and see if he was being followed, so he led the paint out and back around the mountain. Stopping every hundred paces or so, he studied his back trail.

Peeking between the boughs of a fir, Jack Vance cursed himself when he saw the boy studying the hindquarter. He should have been more careful about how he took the slice of meat. But it was no matter. The boy had loaded it, and was setting out.

Again, he could feel his purse swelling. At the end of the boy's journey with the meat, there could be another thousand dollars. Even five hundred, only one man, would double the take he was already sure of.

It was a long, slow journey. The boy seemed to hesitate warily at every chance to search the forest behind. But Jack was too clever for him, staying well above, only moving to where he could be seen in the most careful manner. Occasionally he would rein up, dismount, and walk to an edge where he would creep until only his head showed to whoever might be watching from below, and study the mountainside below until he could see the boy, or until the youth and paint came back into view. He was a clever little wolf whelp, but not clever enough.

Vance knew that a man studies his back trail, normally looking behind and below if he's climbing, seldom above. If he lost the boy completely, he could drop down and pick up his trail, but would only do so as a last resort.

Tom was moving slowly, but steadily. He had spent the morning cleaning up the cave, and packing and rolling his gear behind the saddle of his old mule. It had been all he could do to heft the saddle in place on the mule, and he was thankful that the faithful old mule had stood quietly while being loaded.

When he'd first awakened in the cave, he'd been so sick he could think of little else, but in the few days he'd been there, the wound in his side had closed nicely, and Roan had been a fine nurse, making sure Tom was well fed, warm, and dry. Tom still had to favor the side, and was still weak as a two-minute colt, but he was on the mend.

He owed the boy.

Where was Dan McKeag? Had the bastards managed to kill Dan as well? Were he and Roan the only ones left connected with the Lucky Seven?

Roan had seen no sign of anyone on the mountain, other than those riding for the Bar X brand — and they wouldn't have been so bold had Dan or the others been around. Roan had gone back a couple of days after they'd been bushwhacked, and found and buried Slim John's remains. It had been a grisly job, as Roan had reported, as a black bear and other critters had already been at John. But he'd managed, as he'd managed so much else while Tom had been so laid up he couldn't function.

Tom was a long way from right, but he was well enough to ride, and he meant to ride straight to find Marshal Greenlaw and see that Prager and the Bar X boys were taken to task. Hopefully, to task with the business end of a hemp rope, but he truly wondered if that would ever happen.

Prager was a powerful man, and seemed to own everyone of influence and power in the territory. Everyone except Marshal Houston Greenlaw. But what could Greenlaw do if the politicians and judges were against him? Very little, Tom feared. He knew what it was like to be at the mercy of hard, ruthless men who had the law on their side. He'd run from it years ago when he came to Montana to escape slavery.

He was sitting on a rock outside the rift to the cave, when he saw Roan approach from across the draw. Roan stopped on the crest before descending and studied his back trail for a long while, then came on.

"You're a careful soul," Tom said. "I'm right proud of you."

"I hope so. Got the rest of the elk, but I had to wait till an old griz she-bear and her two 'most-grown cubs finished with the gut pile."

"And?" Tom said, noting the worried look on the boy's face.

"And someone took a whack out of this hindquarter," he said, unloading it.

"A critter?"

"Nope. I'd say a sharp knife, and I had it well up in a fir tree. They had to lower it, then raise it again."

"That's why you were watching your back trail so careful."

"It was. I wouldn't of come back here at all, till after dark, 'cept you said you wanted to get started down the mountain."

"Go inside and fetch my Winchester, and I'll sit and gander your back trail while you load up the rest of your stuff. Pack up the rest of the back strap, and we'll leave these quarters hanging in the cave, in case we have to come back and hide out some more."

Roan led the paint into the cave, and set about his task, while Tom kept a lookout at his back trail.

Jack Vance was confounded and confused. He'd watched the boy go into a mixed grove of aspens and firs, seen the black man awaiting him, and then the boy had disappeared. Just poofed away, like a wisp of smoke or a spirit.

Finally he decided there must be a hole in the rock face near where the old man sat gazing off down the mountain. Maybe even a cave. He was sure the boy had disappeared into the mountain, but was there someone else there also? Was the man they called Slim John somewhere inside?

He decided to drop down the hillside and take the old man unawares. Vance knew Old Man Prager wanted them dead, but he'd want to see the bodies before he paid up. Jack Vance had hauled dead men before, and knew it was a damn sight easier to travel with live men than dead; deadweight was a hard, clumsy load to strap on a horse. And some horses didn't take to having dead things of any kind on their back, even men they were used to hauling. Jack was in no mood for a rodeo on a steep mountainside. He was alone, and that black man looked more than two hundred pounds. Even with the boy helping to load his body, if he killed the boy last, it would be a job.

He'd take them alive, make them ride down the mountain well tied in the saddle, until he got close to the Bar X, then kill them where they sat and haul them in.

Smiling at the thought, at a good plan, he dismounted, slipped the Winchester from its saddle scabbard, and moved into the fir stand, beginning a careful descent.

Placing every foot as if he was hunting a wary animal — and he was, maybe a pack of them — he moved down the mountain until he was only a few feet from the old man.

Chapter 19

Tom heard the crack of a twig, turning just in time to catch the sun-flash on the barrel as it crashed up against the side of his head. He went down in a heap at the base of the rock.

Jack Vance moved carefully to the elderberry bush, cocked the Winchester and palmed his revolver, then charged into the cave.

He hadn't accounted for the darkness, and it took a moment for his eyes to adjust.

A moment too long.

When Roan, who was packing his bedroll on the paint, realized the man backlighted in the opening wasn't Tom, he dove back into the darkness. The Sharps was in a saddle scabbard, but he wore the LeMat on his hip, and he slapped for it as he scrambled back into the depth of the cave.

A deafening roar ripped down the cave as Vance fired the Winchester after him, but he'd rounded a small turn. The bullet ricocheted off the walls, singing a death song until it disappeared harmlessly into the depths.

Then it was dead silent for a moment, until Vance's voice rang out. "You alone in here, boy?"

"There's fifteen of us," Roan shouted back. His reply was confident, but his voice rang of fear.

"Fifteen, eh?" Jack Vance laughed. "You're quite the joker, boy."

Roan slunk even deeper into the cave, only the quiet padding of his feet heard. He decided silence was best.

"So, this old black boy out here an amigo of your'un?"

Still, Roan made no sound.

"I didn't kill the old boy, just clubbed him down. He'll be fine, unless . . ."

Silence.

"But I think I'm gonna have to put a slug in his ugly head bone should you not come on out."

Fear surged anew through Roan.

"Mr. Prager wants to have a talk with you, boy. He don't want you shootin' at no surveyors or Bar X boys no more. Then you can go on your way."

"I ain't got nowhere to go," Roan yelled.

"I got me some dynamite in my saddlebags. I'm just gonna have to shoot the old man, then I'm gonna blow this cave mouth and put a hundred tons of rock down. You ready to die a long slow death sealed in a tomb, boy?"

Roan was silent a moment, thinking about this turn of events. Now he desperately wished he'd explored the depths of the cave and seen if there was another outlet . . . but he hadn't. Finally, he tried to negotiate. "You let Tom go, and I'll come on out."

"He's having his'sef a nap. He couldn't go nowhere if I poked him with a stick."

"What do you want with us?"

"Old Man Prager just wants you off the place. I'm to invite you down to the ranch. After you have a chat and a glass of lemonade, you're on your way. That is, if'n you don't put up no tussle. If you do, I'm instructed to shoot you down like a dog. But I'm a peaceful man, son. I don't want to do that, even if you are tresspassin' on the Bar X."

"The hell I am. This is Lucky Seven ground."

"Nope, Mr. Prager bought it from Dan McKeag, over in Helena, right before McKeag was shot dead by some bar wench."

"Uncle Dan? Uncle Dan is dead?"

"Dead and buried, boy. Prager owns the Seven now, and all he wants is for you to come on down. Hell, he'll even give you a job, should you come in peaceful-like."

"And if I don't?"

"Then I'm walking outside, shootin' this worthless old buffalo soldier in the head, and blowing up this cave. Ain't worth nothing to nobody but the bats nohow."

"Go to hell."

Vance cackled at that. "I done got me a reservation, boy." Then he sighed deeply, as if he was exasperated. "I guess I got to shoot this old man, then blow you all to hell, before I can get on down to supper."

There was a long silence, then Roan relented. "I'm coming out, but don't you hurt Tom."

"He ain't worth the lead."

"I'm coming out. I got this revolver by the barrel."

"Then come on."

Vance made Roan help him lift Tom up into the mule's saddle, just as he was beginning to regain his senses. Then he made Roan mount the paint. Vance tied them both into the saddle, binding their hands to the saddle horns and tying their legs to the cinches so they were fixed firmly in place.

He tail-tied the paint to the mule, and took up the mule's lead rope to lead the pair, then set off down the mountain, riding in silence.

All Roan could think of was his Uncle Dan. He couldn't believe that Dan sold the Lucky Seven, nor that it was possible that Dan was dead. Could it be?

He wanted to cry, but fourteen-year-old boys — young men — didn't cry.

Still, his throat burned, and he wanted to.

Dan and Pad had followed the trail until they found where an animal had been butchered, then set out following the trail of a single horse leading away around the mountain.

They reined up short, hearing a strange gunshot, close, but echoing, as if it had been shot down a well.

"Where was that?" Dan asked as Blue barked in reply, but Dan shushed him.

"I dunno," Paddy said, cupping a hand to his ear, but no shot followed. "It sounded close and far. Strange. Damned if I know."

"Let's push it some harder. I got a strange tickle in my spine . . . something's close and wrong."

They moved at a rapid walk where the trail was worst, and a trot or canter where it got better. Twice, Dan lost the track of the hunter, one time working up and down the slope until he found another trail higher than the first. Blue was no tracking hound, but he did have a fine nose, and worked it hard, helping Dan time and again to locate the trail. Dan was surprised to see he was back on the trail of the man riding the horse with the nick in the rear shoe, and it seemed as if one or the other of the two tracks might be trailing, or pacing, the other. He couldn't tell which, as both were recent trails.

He decided to trail the hunter, convinced that the second trail was moving along with the first. The hunter was riding a small horse. Roan's paint was a small horse, and that had convinced him to follow the hunter. He hoped against all hope that the hunter was his nephew, Roan.

It took an hour for him to find the cave, and dried blood on the rock just outside the opening. Circling the cave opening, Dan checked for sign, then went inside.

Dan quickly searched the cave, following and depending upon Blue, while Pad rode to a nearby overlook and studied the canyon below, Spotted Dog Creek Canyon. Dan and the big dog exited and Dan waved Paddy back over. "Somebody's been here for some time. There's a whitetail hanging back in that cave that's been carved on for a good while. There's jerky drying on a willow rack near a still-smoldering fire, and the strips are good and dry. Looks like two of them. One of them's wearing moccasins. Tom wears moccasins most times."

"You think the other could be Roan?"

"Could well be. And there's a third man — the man who spent the night down at the barn.

"I think Roan was the hunter we've been following, Tom was here with him. The third man joined up with them. It might be Slim John, but I don't think so. Whoever it was, the three of them rode out together."

"Why not Slim John?"

"The horse with the nick is a steady walker. John always picked a wild one out of the string. He strutted like the cock of the walk, and wanted his mount to do the same. I've seen John on a lot of rank stock that humped like French whores — kept their head lower than their hind hoofs about half the time — and don't believe I ever saw light under Slim John's butt. He stuck to a saddle like no man I ever saw.

His mounts were a lot of things, but steady walker wasn't among them."

"Then who?"

"I don't know, but let's get down the trail after them and find out."

They sat out at the same hard pace they'd kept up before finding the cave, but this time downhill, the horses often slipping and sliding.

When they reached the bottom of the mountain, with the horses well lathered, Blue falling behind, the trail flattened out through a meandering grove of cottonwoods, and they began a steady trail-eating lope.

"Dismount!" Jack Vance yelled, hearing the hoofbeats on the trail behind them. He leapt from the saddle, forgetting he'd tied them on so they couldn't dismount. He whipped a long-bladed knife from its scabbard on his waist, and cut away the leather thongs he'd used to tie ankles to cinch, and then unwound their wrist ties and shoved them out of the saddles to crash on the trail below.

Tom had regained some sensibility, but he was courting a terrible headache, and his vision was blurred from the blow.

"Drag him into the brush," Vance commanded. "If y'all try to run, I'll shoot you down like jackrabbits."

Roan nodded and helped Tom, as best he could, to get off the trail into the underbrush.

Vance quickly gathered the horses, and led them into a copse of thick aspens, returned, and knelt behind a fallen cottonwood where he could see the trail for a hundred yards behind their position.

In moments, two riders broke into view, moving fast.

Vance waited until they were only twenty yards from his position, then rose and leveled the muzzle on the man in the lead, riding a blood gelding or stud, wearing a broad-brimmed hat. The man reined up.

"Dan!" the yell came from the brush, where Roan had arisen.

"Dan McKeag," Jack Vance said. "I heared you was done shot dead."

"Who the hell is Dan McKeag?" Dan snapped as Roan bit his tongue. Paddy had reined up behind him, his hand resting on the butt of his revolver.

"Don't touch that iron," Vance said, shifting the muzzle to Paddy. Quickly, his mind raced. If this was really Dan McKeag, and he hadn't been killed in Helena as the boss thought, what would

Prager pay? A thousand. Maybe more.

"You two climb on down." Vance motioned with the muzzle of the rifle. "Wrong side, so's you don't get behind those animals."

"I never wrong-side-dismounted Ol' Lucifer," Paddy said. "He might act up."

"Then he's gonna act up," Vance snapped. "Now do it."

They dismounted on the right-hand side of the animals, in plain view of Vance.

"So, you're Dan McKeag," Vance said, still doubtful.

"I told you, friend, I'm not McKeag. My name is Goodnight. Daniel Goodnight."

"The hell, ain't nobody named Goodnight."

Dan was watching him carefully, wondering if he dare try his left-handed draw. He had to have some advantage, if he expected to come out on top. "If I can fish in my saddlebags," he said, "I can come up with some papers that might make you believe me."

"What are you doin' hereabouts?" Vance asked.

"Heading for Deer Lodge City, to buy some cattle."

"You carrying cattle-buyin' money?" Vance asked. This could be better than he thought. Maybe even better than delivering Dan McKeag to Old Man Prager.

"I got deposit money, not much. Most of it will come by bank draft."

A moan came from Tom in the brush, just beyond where Roan stood.

"Who's hiding out in there?" Dan asked.

"Tom —" Roan said, then remembered Dan was acting like a stranger. "Tom Macklin, who this owlhoot clubbed down with that rifle."

"Shudup, boy." Vance turned back to Dan. "What's not much?"

Dan could hear faint footfalls on the trail behind. This could be the distraction he was looking for.

"A little more than a thousand. If that's what you're after, let me fish it out."

"Remember, I got this .44-40 aimed at your midsection. It'll blow a hole in you that you could drive a surrey through."

Chapter 20

"Just let me get the money," Dan said, reaching over and unbuckling the saddlebag. He fished in with his right hand until he found a sack of Arbuckle's coffee. The footfalls, rattling the fallen cottonwood leaves, were close, almost upon them.

He turned, and Jack Vance's eyes were glued to the cloth sack. "Throw it over," he said.

Dan tossed it, purposely short.

"Back away," Vance ordered, and both Dan and Paddy backed up a couple of steps.

Just as Vance bent to retrieve the sack, Blue pounded into where they all stood in a small clearing.

Jack Vance's eyes flared in terror as he tried to gain his feet and bring the Winchester to bear in one motion. His first thought was a bear had run into camp, then a wolf. Then he realized it was a dog, as big as a wolf, and all snarls and teeth.

"Get him, Blue!" Dan shouted, and the

big slathering dog turned his attention to the only man in the group he didn't know. Vance was raising his rifle at the dog as Blue set his powerful hindquarters and from ten feet away leapt for the man's throat. The Winchester fired, but went wild. Vance was knocked over backward with the force of the more than ninety pounds of Irish wolfhound/wild wolf.

Vance rolled to the side and tried to scramble away, but Blue locked his jaws into the back of the man's thigh. Vance still had the rifle, and was madly trying to jack in another shell.

He did, but just as both Dan and Paddy's revolvers roared. One shot took him in the chest, one just under the eye. He was dead when he hit the ground.

Blue stood over him, his muzzle only inches from the man's bloodied face, growling, making sure the adversary was no longer a danger to his master.

Dan ran to Roan, and the boy met him. Both of them encircled each other with welcoming arms.

"I knew it," Roan said, his head on Dan's big shoulder. "I knew they couldn't kill you, Uncle Dan."

After greetings were over, a fire was built and Tom was made comfortable. While

Paddy buried Jack Vance in a small ravine near the trail, Dan and Roan caught up on what had happened since they'd last seen each other, almost a month before.

And Roan described in detail what had happened at the cabin, and the man who'd actually shot Erin. He knew there were two men, and described them each in fairly good detail. He particularly remembered the man with the scar on his cheek, and he'd shot the other, so he should be carrying a hell of a scar from the LeMatt shotgun barrel.

It had been an eventful, and terrible, month.

They stayed there until morning, until Dan was sure that Tom Macklin could ride. Tom was much better. He still had the headache, but the double vision was gone. And Dan knew he was tough as tanned hide and twice as lasting.

Over coffee, he gave them instructions. "Paddy and I have business over in Missoula, and maybe beyond. I want you and Tom to ride back the way you came, over the mountain, and keep going until you get to Helena."

"I'm going with you, Uncle Dan," Roan said, his eyes filing with tears.

"You've done more than any youngster should have ever had to do, Roan. We've got to ride hard and fast." Dan saw that this line of reasoning was getting him nowhere, so he backtracked. "And I know you could keep up, and I know you're not afraid of anything, and would face down a crazed bull buffalo. God knows you've proved that."

Roan wiped his eyes and smiled.

"But I need you to take care of Tom. And I want you to take Blue back with you. He's getting footsore, and won't be able to keep up. If I can use you on the trail, I'll send for you later, but the first thing is to get Tom safe until he mends . . . and Blue where he can rest up."

"Take care of Tom? And Blue?" Roan said, doubtful.

"Yes. You saved Tom's life, Roan. It would be a terrible waste to let the old boy go toes-up now."

"The hell you say," Tom snapped, but he knew what Dan was up to.

"And I need both of you when we get the ranch back. I can't run it without you. Besides, Erin would want you to take care of Tom and Blue, now that she can't."

Roan nodded. This made sense to him.

"Where do you want us to hole up?" Tom asked.

"There's a lady in Helena, and a saloon named the Bonny Glen."

The trail back to the Mullen Road took them past the ranch. They sat on the hillside looking down on the buildings, and Dan was surprised to see a wagon with hoop canvas covering its contents parked at the place, and three people at the fresh graves, one a child.

He decided he had to see who it was, and rode on down.

Again, folks he knew were shocked to see him. Fresh flowers adorned the graves, and Erin's, which Paddy had marked the last time they were there, had been lined with rocks in a neat and tidy manner. Kelly and Meegan Dugan and their little boy, Kel, had made a special trip on their way back to town, going out of their way to visit Erin's grave.

After Kelly told him he'd quit and why, who Jack Vance was and what he was about, what he knew of the four men, and confirmed that he thought they were heading west, not south, Dan asked, "So, what are you going to do, Kelly?"

"Head into town and see if I can get on somewhere."

"You're a cattleman, Kelly, and a fine

one. You need to keep on ranching. The railroad will be here in a few years, and the cattle business will boom."

"I will hang with it if I can, Dan."

"If I get back — when I get back — and if I get the ranch back so all's legal, you'll have a job on the Lucky Seven. Seems we're down a few hands. And Meegan is a fine cook, if I remember right . . . you can both work, if you're of a mind to."

"You remember right. I could ride with you two," Kelly said. "If you can use the help." Which elicited a hard look from Meegan, who grabbed a handful of his shirtsleeve in a less-than-gentle manner.

Dan smiled appreciatively. "You've got a wife and fine boy to look after, Kelly. We can handle this."

They parted with a handshake, and Dan was glad that Kelly and Meegan had proven to be the friends he'd thought they were.

It took two and a half days of hard riding down the Hell Gate River until they came out of the canyon at midday and saw the buildings of Missoula in the distance.

Jack Vance had been a surprise.

The next six wouldn't be.

Dan rode straight to Deputy Marshal Ira Witcomb's office, and presented the letter from Houston Greenlaw. Houston had been generous with the letter, stating that Dan was acting as his agent and as a bounty hunter and that several people who Dan would identify were wanted for attempted murder and murder, and more.

"So, who are these men who are wanted?" the tall thin marshal asked.

Dan gave him Al Givens's name and description.

"Hell, fella with a bad scar on his left cheek. I had him and two of his cohorts in my jail . . . and I understand another is over in the Sisters of Providence."

"Church?"

"Nope, hospital. Got his leg sawed off."

"But not now?"

"The one in at Sisters is still there. The rest rode out of town, and good riddance to 'em."

"You got some names for me?"

For the first time, Dan learned the names of all four men. Then he asked, "And the woman?"

"A woman!"

"Yes, wanted for attempted murder," Dan said, stretching the truth, as there was no formal warrant for the woman — but she was damn sure wanted by Dan. "She goes by Shelaugh, and runs with a no-good name of Brown, big fella who uses the handle Brownie." This was information Dan had gleaned from Shelaugh's former employer, Rose Ballard.

On the way over, he'd spent a lot of time thinking about the woman. Could he shoot down a woman, even if it was merely returning the favor? He wondered. He sure as hell could in self-defense, and no one would condemn him for it.

But he sure as hell meant to find her, and then he'd let the chips fall where they may. Almost before he finished the thought, the marshal offered, "There's a new girl over at Headquarter's who goes by the name Shelaugh."

"You don't say. What's Headquarter's?"

"Finest saloon in town. Just over near Higgins on Front Street. You can't miss it. You want I should go over with you?"

Dan was a little quick to reply. "No. No, thanks, Marshal. Mr. Dundee and I can handle this. No need to trouble you."

Witcomb seemed to ponder this a moment, then shrugged. "I got a ton of paperwork here." Then he looked hard into Dan's eyes. "Don't be shootin' up my town, McKeag."

"No, sir. Wouldn't think of it."

Dan excused himself.

"We're in luck," he told Paddy. "There's a woman goes by Shelaugh just took a bar-girl job at a local joint. We might as well start there."

Two blocks away they reined up in front of one of the town's most imposing buildings. A dray wagon was unloading beer kegs in front of the place, and the rail was lined with horses. The Headquarter's was a busy place, even in the afternoon.

Dan and Paddy went in separately. Paddy walked to the far end of the long bar, lined with drovers and miners and townsmen. Dan stopped near the bat-wing doors, where he could eye the whole place. There were only two women in the place, one a blonde who stood at the bar, enticing a couple of miners, and he couldn't quite make out the other one at a table in the darkened rear — but she had dark hair, he could see that much. She sat with a man in a bowler hat, much like the one Paddy wore.

The bartender came over, mopping beer from a handlebar mustache with a towel. "New batch of beer in, and it's fine," he said.

"Whiskey. Irish, if you have it."

"I do," he said, reaching under the bar and pulling an unlabeled bottle up.

"Nope, the good stuff," Dan said, figuring the unlabeled was made down the road somewhere.

The bartender shrugged. "The good stuff is a quarter a shot."

"The good stuff."

While the bartender poured, Dan asked, "I've got an old friend in town, a girl named Shelaugh."

The man smiled broadly. "Hell, you're in luck. She's back there right now. Don't let that fella she's with concern you . . . he's a regular."

"Brownie."

"You know old Brownie? He's with her. Brownie comes on at six p.m., he's a dealer here. You ought to try your luck."

"You know, I believe I will," he said, but he didn't mean at the tables.

Dan downed the drink in a swallow, then headed directly for the table in the rear where Shelaugh and her beau, big Brownie, sat. He nodded to Paddy on the way past. Paddy merely turned and leaned back against the bar, but Dan noticed that he casually hoisted and dropped his revolver.

The girl was dressed in saloon-girl attire, with a knee-length dress cut low on top and high on bottom, with knit stockings.

She had a reticule hanging on the back of the chair, and it might have held a knife or belly gun. The man was in shirtsleeves with a garter on each sleeve. He wore no belt and holster, and if he was armed, it wasn't where it could be seen.

Dan moved as if he was heading for the back door, and out to the privy, but turned at the last second and slipped into a seat across from the pair. They were only three paces from Paddy at the bar.

Shelaugh flashed him a smile, then the smile turned down at the ends. "My God . . ." she managed.

"Nope, just me, Shelaugh. You'd do better facing God."

"Who?" Brownie asked, his eyes shifting back and forth from Shelaugh, who was white in the face, to Dan, whose expression didn't encourage him to smile and extend a hand.

Dan flashed him a hard look. "Dan McKeag, Mr. Brown. You remember that name. You were among the louts who were supposed to shoot me down."

Brownie was awestruck. He merely stared, trying to comprehend what was being said.

Shelaugh collected herself. "We was just working for a living, Mr. McKeag." Then she smiled nervously. "Truth is, I'm real glad to see you seeming so well off."

"Not real glad, lass. I'm hoping you'll be trying again to send me to the maker, this time while I know the worth of you and will be ready."

As he spoke, he could see Brownie's shoulder dip slightly. He was reaching for his ankle.

"Brownie," Dan said harshly, "I hear you're a gambling man. When this game's over, you won't even have your tail feathers."

"What?" Brownie said, hesitating.

"I've got all the cards, Brownie."

Chapter 21

Brownie smiled a tight hard smile, but continued to reach.

Dan, unseen by the other two, had pulled the revolver in his left hand as he sat, and had it leveled at the big man under the table.

"Look out," Paddy yelled as Brownie jerked upright.

He didn't get the little single-shot boot gun aimed before Dan's Remington roared, and big Brownie was blown back against the wall, a very surprised look on his face.

Shelaugh screamed, and dug into the reticule, but Paddy stepped quickly forward and cracked her across the wrist with the barrel of his revolver. She screamed even louder and dropped the bag, rubbing her wrist with the other hand.

Dan rose, stepped over, and removed the small gun from Brownie's big clenched fist. Brownie was rolling back and forth in agony, grasping his belly, now with both hands.

"You're gut-shot, Mr. Brown," Dan said. "I believe you're gonna die hard. Big fella like you is an easy target."

"Put that down," Dan heard Paddy say, and turned to see Paddy's revolver leveled at the bartender, who was holding a scattergun that he'd fished out from behind the bar. He didn't have it leveled yet, pointing still at the tin sculptured ceiling.

His mustache twitched as he was making up his mind. Then Paddy spoke again. "You can go to hell with your dealer here, who is wanted by the law, or you can drop that to the floor."

"It's cocked, it'll discharge and blow me leg off."

"Then uncock it, while it's still aiming at the ceiling, and drop it." Paddy extended his arm holding the revolver at length, so he was aiming dead at the middle of the bartender's chest.

The bartender did as he was told. The double clattered on the floor behind the bar.

Shelaugh saw that both Dan and Paddy's attention was turned to the bartender, and took the opportunity to bolt for the back door. In one step, Paddy had her by her long black tresses. She kept running, but her head jerked back and her upper body stayed where Paddy held her. Her feet flew out and she fell on her butt on the barroom floor, among the peanut shells. She began to cry.

Paddy bent over her. "I wouldn't be moving if I was you, lass. Mr. McKeag here is looking for any opportunity to ventilate your pretty hide."

She lay still, except for bringing her hands to her face and sobbing loudly.

Most of the men at the bar had broken for the front doors and were long gone, but a pair of hard-looking miners moved toward Dan and Paddy.

"That's a woman you're moppin' the floor with," one of them said.

"If you have business with her," Dan said, cocking and leveling the Remington at the approaching pair, "you can visit her in the jailhouse. She's wanted, and she's going there, and if you want to go along, or go to the undertaker, take another step."

They hesitated, then they too spun on their heels and headed for the door.

Dan walked over and bent over the prostrate woman, who was wailing loudly. He placed the muzzle of the Remington on her forehead.

"No! No!" she screamed.

"I believe you're a candidate for hell's

fires, you rotten bitch," Dan said and, in an exaggerated manner, pulled the trigger.

She screamed and fainted, as Paddy about did.

The hammer had fallen on the empty chamber, which Dan had adjusted it to on his way to accost her.

Paddy began to laugh. "Damn, if that wasn't a jaw dropper. I got to admit, I was surprised as a hot hound trying to poke a porcupine."

"I thought it was just fine, and hope it gives her nightmares for the rest of her worthless days," Dan said, flashing Paddy a rather satisfied grin. "Sling her over your shoulder and let's tote her over to the jailhouse."

Paddy laughed again, and shouldered her easily.

When she awoke, she was sure she wasn't in heaven. They'd hung a blanket up in the cell so she could use the chamber pot with some privacy. Later, while she sat on a cold metal bunk, Dan questioned her about the others, but she refused to answer. "There's nothing in it for me," she said. She rose and walked to stare out the window.

"Oh. How about stretching that pretty neck in front of a bunch of jeering hoora'n men. You're a dance hall Mary, but I'll bet you never danced on air. Hell, woman, I saw an old boy about your size drop, and his head snapped clean off. How would you like to go to your maker with your head tucked under one arm and with your tongue hanging out like a coal-mine mule . . . or then again, maybe you wouldn't like that."

She sobbed for a moment, then looked up. "They don't hang women," she said, then looked doubtful. "Do they?"

"Women are coming into their own, Shelaugh. Hell, they even got the vote here in Montana. I believe a good jury of good Christian menfolk would relish the chance to hang a no-good, lying, cheating, low-down, evil whore like yourself."

She was silent for a long moment, not being used to being talked to like that, even if it was true. Finally, she asked in a quiet voice, "Could you keep that from happening? Would you?"

"I'm sure I could. I'm the one you shot. I could say I reached for the gun, tried to grab it, and you really didn't mean to shoot me. You might do jail time, but you damn sure deserve that. Would I? Now that's a different pot of beans altogether. Thing is, I'll help you avoid the thirteen turns, but I want the truth, a signed statement, and your word you'll tell it to a jury, should it come to that."

In moments, Dan sent Paddy to the Western Union office, where he hired the operator, who was the fastest man in town with a pen. For over an hour, Dan asked questions, and Shelaugh answered. By the time he left, he had a four-page signed statement, implicating the other four as accomplices in his shooting, and more importantly to Dan, implicating Bert Prager. She knew nothing of what had happened at the Lucky Seven, to Erin and the others, but it was a start.

She also knew that Al Givens had ridden south, to Stevensville, and Badger and Slater north, to Demersville, on the Flathead River.

Brownie died in the doctor's office before they rode out of town. Dan paid the doctor a five-dollar gold piece, and then the undertaker a ten-dollar one. He considered it some of the best money he'd ever spent.

When that business was concluded, they headed for Sisters of Providence Hospital, and the first of the next four men on his list. But this time, with Marshal Ira Whitcomb in tow. Dan wouldn't have included him, but he knew he couldn't shoot a man who was still in a hospital bed just having had a leg lopped off — much as he might want to. Instead, they left the hospital with Dutch Blodget chained to the bed, having instructed the nuns that Ira was to be notified when the man could be transferred to the jail.

Dan did take the time to tell Dutch who he was, and that it was a pity Dutch might not have enough weight to snap his neck when the trapdoor fell, with the missing leg and all. Dan informed him, "If your neck don't break, I'll be along to give you a couple of tugs to make sure it snaps."

Dutch cursed the boy who'd shot him, and Dan made a mental note to treat the boy to something special.

Before they left the hospital, Dan made sure Dutch knew good and clear what faced him. "Blodget, I know you're the man who shot down the best woman to ever grace this territory. I'm gonna see you hang, and I'm gonna make sure it's a slow, terrible death. You think about that, and I'll be back."

"I didn't shoot no woman. I was there, but I didn't shoot no woman."

They forded the Hell Gate River late in the afternoon, deciding to camp wherever they ran out of light.

"What?" Paddy asked as he heard Dan say something as they were riding south along the Bitterroot River, toward Stevensville and Fort Owen.

"Just having a little chat with your sis."

"So, what about?"

"Thought she'd like to know, three down, three to go — if we don't count Old Man Prager. But then, he's special — least, I believe he thinks he is. I plan to show him he's common as dirt, and to put six feet of it in his face."

Fat Anton Auchenbach was enjoying his time in Stevensville. He traded with the Salish, sold whiskey, produce, feed, and dry goods, and generally was making out just fine. He'd held on to his little trading post turned general merchandise store for ten years, since he'd come to the valley after the "recent unpleasentries," as the war was called by those in his hometown of Fredericksburg, Texas.

His store consisted of a single-story log building, backed up by a tall barn with a hayloft. The store fronted on Stevensville's block-long main street. Fat Anton traded horses and sold tack and feed out of the barn — and let the occasional traveler sleep in the hayloft. He didn't charge those for the sleeping quarters, if they traded in the store and boarded their horses for a quarter dollar a night.

Al Givens didn't have to pay even that, as he was an old friend of Anton's, having served in the war with Anton under Major General Sterling Price, and having escaped with Anton after being separated from the main force at the Battle of Little Blue River. Anton had been his sergeant when Givens took a ball to the face that resulted in the ugly scar.

That separation from the rest of their company gave them leave to desert and find their way back to Texas, where Givens lived on the Auchenbach farm for most of a bad winter. Private Al Givens and Sergeant Anton Auchenbach got crossways with the local law, and lit out for points north just after the war, at about the time questions were being asked about how they'd come to leave Price's forces.

Stevensville had a dozen buildings, none of which were as impressive as Auchenbach's.

It was early in the afternoon when Dan and Paddy rode past Fort Owen and approached the little town built on the banks of the Bitterroot River.

"I think we'll ride in separate again,

Paddy," Dan said. "That worked out right good in Missoula."

"Agreed. You or me first?"

Dan fished in his pocket and pulled out a coin. "Heads or tails," he said, flipping.

"Heads," Paddy said.

"You're first," Dan said. "I'll meet you at the saloon, if there is one. Or the general store if not."

"I won't drink all the whiskey."

"You'd best not, as I'm dry as a four-score old widow woman."

Dan gave him twenty minutes, then followed. As he'd guessed, there was no saloon, but there was a general store, and printed in small letters under the main sign, it said CAFÉ AND SALOON.

Dan entered to see Paddy, to his right, leaning on a bar in a side room separated from a large room by low bat-wing doors, a bar with only six stools. To his left was a door out of the store marked PRIVATE. He presumed it was living quarters. The store was stacked high with dry goods and farm implements, barrels of grain and pickles and potatoes, and bolts of cloth. Furs hung from the walls, as did the traps to take them. Paddy was upending a whiskey. There were three tables also. At one of them, three men sat playing cards, and one more man was leaning on the bar, at the far end from Paddy.

And that man had a scar on his left cheek, porkchop sideburns, and sandy blond unkempt hair. Dan could feel the heat begin to crawl up his backbone.

Dan made note of the fact that Paddy had brought his shotgun into the store with him, and it leaned against the bar beneath him.

Smoke hung in the room, as the cardplayers were all smoking cigars, and Fat Anton had a pipe hanging from his heavy lips.

Dan presumed the huge man behind the bar was Fat Anton, as he was not only tall, but had a girth like a horse. He mopped his forehead, then his bald head, with a bar towel as Dan approached.

"Damn if this ain't turning out to be a busy day," the big man said.

Dan nodded, walked to the bar, ordered a whiskey, and went to a table in the corner where he could keep his back to the wall and see both the bar and the cardplayers.

"So," Paddy said, handing his glass to the big man for a refill, "what's this here Stevensville all about?"

"Just a friendly little town," the big man

said. "We got a mill down on the river, and there's a few dozen farms in the valley." Then he extended a hand to Paddy. "I be Anton Auchenbach," he said in a low gruff voice.

Paddy shook with him. "Paddy Dundee, Mr. Auchenbach. You'd be the proprietor of this fine establishment?"

"I would," he replied with a wide smile. "What brings you here?"

"It sure ain't the women," Paddy said, looking around the room, then guffawing.

"It wouldn't be that," Fat Anton said, agreeing. "Then . . . what?"

"Just passin' through, friend."

"From where, going where?" Anton pressed.

Paddy was silent for a moment. "You must be keepin' the log on this here boat."

Anton gave him a tight smile. "Nope, no log. Just interested. You see, Mr. Dundee, I'm also the law hereabouts. It's my job to know who's about, and what they're about. Don't you know."

Paddy laughed. "Hell, I thought Ira Whitcomb down in Missoula was the territorial marshal on this side of the country."

"He is, but we're a town here, and we figure we got a right to appoint our own law, since Whitcomb is so far and gone."

"Well, here's to you, lawman," Paddy said, upending the drink again.

Anton merely nodded. He didn't seem to like how this conversation was going. Paddy held out the glass for another.

"So, where are you from, Mr. Dundee, and where are you heading?"

"To hell, no doubt," Paddy said with a wide grin.

But Anton didn't return it. "I don't serve men who are ashamed of where they've been, and afraid to tell where they're going, so if you want another, Mr. Dundee, you'll answer me."

Dan winced, fully expecting Paddy to reach across the bar and snatch the big man by his collar, and maybe put a thumb in his eye, but was surprised when Paddy merely winked. "You fill it up, me lad, and I'll tell you about Paddy Dundee."

Fat Anton looked suspicious, but filled it again. Paddy took a sip, then began to sing in a beautiful tenor:

Listen, gentle stranger, I'll read my
    pedigree;
I'm known for handling tenderfeet,
    and worser men than thee;
The lions on the mountains, I've drove
    them to their lairs;

The wildcats are my playmates, I've
    wrestled grizzly bears.

Anton was looking disgusted, but Paddy
continued, even raising his volume for the
chorus:

I'm wild and woolly and full of fleas,
And never curried below the knees.
Now, fat stranger, if you'll give me
    your address —
How would you like to go, by fast mail
    or express?

"Ain't funny," Anton said, his look sour.
The man at the end of the bar, with
fuzzy porkchop sideburns, stepped closer
to Paddy. "Friend, I'd suggest you speak
up and answer Anton's question. We could
ride you out on a rail, mouthy as you are."

Chapter 22

"And you, friend," Paddy said, "are lettin' your alligator mouth overload your hummingbird butt. Your jaw's gonna chafe yer chest, you keep flappin' it."

The man did not step forward within reach of Paddy, but rather stepped back and laid his hand on the butt of the revolver on his hip.

"Al, I can handle this," Anton said, cautioning the man.

Hearing that, getting confirmation that the man was Al Givens, Dan rose and stepped forward. "Gentlemen, gentlemen," Dan said, his arms spread wide as if to embrace them all. He wore a smile, a devilish one, but it was because he'd found the man who'd shot Erin. "This is a fine day. Much too fine to fill the clear air with lead."

"Speakin'," Anton said, "of who and what, just who the devil are you and where are you headed?"

Dan gave him a wide smile, all the time moving closer to Al Givens. He didn't know the man, had never seen him, but the description fit, and Al Givens was known to be a friend of Fat Anton Auchenbach. He wasn't ready to shoot the man down, but he knew enough for what he was about to do.

"Why, friend, I'm just your everyday dead man."

Anton furrowed his heavy eyebrows, and Givens looked at him like he was loony.

But it was all the time Dan needed. He was close enough. He brought the left from down low, and caught the man called Al on the point of his chin with a crack that snapped his head back. The man wind-milled back against the wall, his eyes rolled up in his head, and he slumped down it.

To Dan's great surprise, Fat Anton came over the bar with a vault like a whitetail deer jumping a fence into the garden. And he had a small bat in hand.

Paddy caught him with a hard right in the midsection as he landed, and Anton "ooffed," and doubled, but didn't go down. Dan took the invitation, and kicked hard, planting a boot in the middle of the big man's face. His head snapped up, his eyes rolled back, and he went to his knees, but he managed to grab onto Paddy, who'd stepped in close, flailing with both fists, smack, smack, smack, against the sides of the big man's head. Anton had him by the legs, and sucked him in close.

Dan stepped back for another hard kick, but caught a fist to the side of the head and spun away, his back to the wall. The other three, obviously friends of Anton's, had joined in. One of them went for Paddy, who was being held in place by the big store owner, whose head was still snapping back and forth with blows, and the other two were throwing fists at Dan.

His right arm was still very weak, but his left was stronger than ever. He had his back to the wall, but couldn't throw and block blows fast enough to fend them both off. He caught one beside the head, knocking him back, but kicked the other man hard enough to make him give ground. They tried to close again, and he dove behind the bar, then scrambled to the other side and came up with a bottle full of whiskey in hand, ready to use it for a bludgeon, just as a shot thundered through the small room.

Everything quieted as the echo reverberated, and dust motes wafted down from the log roof.

He rose to see a woman standing between the partially opened bat-wing doors.

A big woman. Looking even larger than she was with a smoking scattergun in hand.

"Now you all stop this foolishness," she demanded, and her demands deserved consideration as she'd only fired one barrel of the double-barrel she held, and she'd lowered the muzzle to scan the room.

"Gerta," Anton said sheepishly, trying to get his head to stop rolling back and forth, and his eyes to focus. "These here fellas started this row."

"The hell," Paddy said, then grabbed his derby, still tight on his head, and held it against his chest with both hands. Anton had let him go with the roar of the gunshot, and the worst Paddy suffered was bleeding knuckles. "Pardon, ma'am," Paddy said contritely. "But that fella over there would be the one who started this fracas."

Al Givens was coming around, trying to get to his feet.

"What do you want we should do with them, Gerta?" one of the other men asked, mopping the blood from his mouth.

"Lock 'em in the tater cellar till the circuit judge comes."

Dan would have none of it, and as he was partially blocked by Anton, stepped forward, drawing his revolver as he did. He clamped an arm around the man's fat neck and shoved the muzzle up against Anton's ear, looking over the man's wide shoulder at his wife. "You won't be locking us anywhere. Ma'am, now you set that shotgun down, so I don't have to blow Fat Anton's head off and muss up your floor."

She looked uncertain, then said why. "Ya know, I been with that fat smelly old man for a half-dozen years, and I might give you a case of whiskey should you blow his ugly head off."

"Gerta," Anton yelled, sounding a little hurt.

"Ma'am," Dan said, cocking the revolver, causing Anton's eyes to go wide. "I'm serious."

She sighed deeply, but didn't set the shotgun aside. "I suppose you're here to rob the place?"

"No, ma'am," Dan said, deadly serious, then lied. "I'm here with a warrant for that man over there." He motioned with his head to where Al Givens had regained his feet.

"Why . . . why didn't you say so," Gerta said with a shrug, and set the shotgun aside. Paddy brushed himself off, then reached across the bar and poured himself another three fingers of whiskey. He fished out his own revolver, and let it hang loosely as his side.

"You can have this freeloader," Gerta said, "but not my whiskey. You didn't earn it. Be putting money on the bar, if'n you'll be drinkin.'" Paddy guffawed, but promptly flipped a silver coin onto the bar top.

"Who the hell are you?" Al Givens asked, his senses returning. The other three who'd been playing cards were returning their chairs and table to the upright position, and licking their wounds.

Dan studied Al Givens. "You don't want to know, Mr. Givens."

"You said you were here for me?"

"And I am, Givens. You see, I'm Dan McKeag. You and the scum you run with murdered my innocent wife and friends."

Givens was taken aback, but not for long. "I didn't kill no woman. Dutch Blodget did the shootin', ask the boy." Then he realized he'd said more than he meant to. He climbed to his feet. "I been right here for more'n three weeks. I didn't shoot no woman." His look hardened. "You might be here for me, McKeag, but your pissin' in the wind if you think you're takin' me anywheres. I ain't never gonna see the inside of some flea-bit jail again."

Dan smiled. "Why, Mr. Givens, I don't figure on takin' you anywhere. I figure on leaving you right here in Stevensville. I passed a nice little cemetery on my way in. If they'd allow scum like you to be planted there. Otherwise, I'll just leave you out in the mud for the crows to pick."

Givens stared at him another moment, then reached for his gun. Dan wasn't faster with his left hand, but he was a lot more steady. Givens's shot cut a groove in Dan's side, but Dan's, a blink later, took Givens dead center in the chest.

He looked very surprised, dropping the revolver as he again was slammed against the wall by the big slug. Then he slumped slowly to the floor, painting the logs with a trail of blood from the exit wound.

Dan scanned the others with the Remington. "Anybody else a fine friend of scum-suckin' woman-killin' Al Givens?"

No one moved, much less spoke.

Finally, Anton spoke up. "He didn't do the shootin', McKeag. This fella Blodget shot the woman. Al told me all about it."

Dan shrugged. "They'll all pay." Then he walked over and patted Givens down as his last breaths rattled in his chest. He jerked up the man's shirt and loosed a cloth money belt, then thumbed through it. "Almost fourteen hundred in here . . . blood money. Hell, I never realized how much I was worth." He stuffed the cloth belt under his leather one, then reached deep into his pocket and fished out a five-dollar gold piece. He flipped it to Gerta, who stood white as death and stark still. She let it hit her in the chest and fall to the floor.

She looked perplexed, and it was turning to anger. "That no-good said he was flat broke. We was lettin' him stay for nothin'. . . ."

Dan nodded to her. "Don't let it be said that Dan McKeag is a freeloader, Miss Gerta."

"It's Mrs. Auchenbach."

"Then, Mrs. Auchenbach, that five dollars is to bury him. Now, I got another ten dollars for you."

"What for?" She looked suspicious.

"For the loan of a pen and ink, and for your husband witnessing what I'm about to write."

"And that is?" she asked, still suspicious.

"The circumstances of Al Givens's death, and his witnessing that fact."

"For ten dollars, hell, yes," she said, now smiling.

Dan wrote the document and Anton

Auchenbach signed it. As an afterthought, Dan had one of the others sign as witness, and bought a bottle for the table. What he didn't tell them was the fact the document was worth two thousand dollars, the reward for Givens dead or alive.

"Now, if you'll sell us a bottle of good whiskey so we can celebrate, we'll be on our way."

"He owed us for room and board, for him and his horse. And there's blood all over my wall and floor."

Dan fished in his pocket, produced another five-dollar gold piece, and flipped it to her. This one she caught handily. "Bury him in the barn, so the livestock can piss on his grave every day."

Paddy began to sing again:

I'm a snorter and a snoozer,
I'm a whiskey abuser. . . .

Then he laughed, and continued:

But he's a killer and a hater,
He's the great annihilator!

He laughed again, and backed out of the bar. Gerta followed him, fetched a bottle of Who Hit John for Paddy, and collected her six bits. Dan snatched up a towel from under the bar and carried it with him, stuffing it under his shirt to soak up blood from the groove Givens's bullet had cut, then watched the others until they both backed out of the store.

"You had me a mite worried there — you gonna need some stitchin' up?" Paddy asked as they mounted.

"Nope. It's more blister than slice. It'll scab over, given a little time."

"Hell, what's one more scar. You look like a cheap carpetbag now, what's been sewed and patched. . . ."

In moments, they were riding hard back toward Missoula.

"Two to go," Paddy yelled at Dan as they loped along.

"Two of the worst, if I hear right. These two may not be so easy — then it's after the herd bull, and he's got two dozen backing him up. We'll soon find out if they ride for the brand."

But it didn't faze Paddy. He began singing in a beautiful tenor again.

They rode the thirty miles to Missoula straight through, arriving in time for breakfast. Both horses were spent, as were the men, but neither would admit it. Finally

Dan had to relent and let them hole up in the livery stable for a few hours. They did, then revisited Shelaugh, and were surprised to see Dutch Blodget in the cell next to her, his leg well bandaged and propped up on the bunk.

The sight of the man set Dan's blood to boiling again, but he was still a one-legged cripple.

"Al Givens said you were the one who shot my wife. Is that true?"

Blodget glared at him for a long moment. "She was shootin' at me, and the boy shot me so's I lost my leg."

"She was shooting at some scum who'd ridden in, accepted a cool drink of water, then killed a better man than the two of you ever thought of being."

Dan slipped his revolver from its holster, cocked it, and aimed it mid-center at the seated Blodget.

"You'd shoot me right here in the jailhouse?" Blodget asked, suddenly looking sicker than ever.

"Gut-shoot you, so you'll die slow and hard."

"Mr. McKeag." The voice rang out authoritatively from the door into the marshal's office. It was Marshal Ira Whitcomb, his arms folded, leaning against the doorjamb. "I'd sure understand, but I'd still have to put you under arrest, and it'd be you standing before the circuit judge looking at a rope."

"It might be worth it," Dan said, never taking his eyes off Blodget.

"Go ahead," Blodget said. "I'm gonna hang anyways."

Dan smiled, and let the hammer down. "You are, and God willin' and the creek don't rise, I'll be here to watch them send you off to eternal pain and damnation. You spend a lot of time thinking about that, Blodget."

Dan was frustrated with the fact of it, but he guessed hanging would have to do. It wasn't as good as killing him with his own hands, but the cards fell where they fell.

With the frustration of not being able to shoot Blodget down and watch him die, Dan was even more driven. He could smell the blood of the other two; smell the end of this rocky trail he'd been riding since being shot down in the alley next to the Bonny Glen. He knew it would end on the Bar X, and the lead that had flown so far was just a preview of what might come, what must come.

He wondered about Rose Ballard, and if

Tom and young Roan had tied up with her, so he took the time to go to Western Union and send a wire, carefully wording it.

Miss Ballard,
Did my package arrive? I'd appreciate your taking care of all until my return. I'm in your debt again. Please answer to P.D. in Demersville, Montana. God willing, we should complete our business there.

D.

Dan bought two tough mountain horses, deciding Dancer and Lucifer would break down if they pushed them on another leg of the journey. Instead, they rode the others and led the two that had carried them so well from Stevensville all the way to Missoula.

Wanting to slow down for the horses' sake, he agreed to walking a mile, loping a mile. He had to make time, for Shelaugh had remembered something else Badger had said. He said he wouldn't mind going on to the Grandmother Country, as the Indians called it — Canada. Dan had to catch them before they crossed into the Grandmother Country. The redcoated

291

mounted police of the neighbor to the north might not be so understanding as Montana marshals.

They pushed hard, to St. Ignatius, and on into the new Salish Reservation.

They camped by some ponds in the Mission Valley, not far from a Salish village. Dan traded a couple of braves two pounds of flour for a fat goose, and they ate their fill before sleeping under the stars.

The next day they came to the lake. Flathead Lake was a place to ponder, but Dan barely slowed down to enjoy the view. He pushed on, up the more easily traveled west side of the lake. They made camp that night on the very north edge of Flathead Lake, only a few miles from Demersville.

Dan was up long before the sun, and had the horses watered and saddled by the time Paddy had rolled up his bedroll.

"You got a real itch," Paddy said.

"I plan to have you bellying up to the Bonny Glen bar in four days or less, but we got business to finish before we ride east."

"We coulda had a little breakfast."

"In Demersville, I'm sure there's a place that feeds those loggers to a fine fettle."

"And miners. They got a new strike, if I hear right, up in the high lonely to the east."

"Whatever. Let's go find a biscuit, and a bucket of blood."

Paddy mounted. "Damned if you wouldn't spoil a fella's appetite."

"I plan to spoil a couple of fellas' appetites, should this day go well."

Chapter 23

They pounded out with the sun just coloring the sky over the high granite mountains to the east, this time back on Dancer and Lucifer, leading the other two.

In less than ten miles, they would be in Demersville.

Now, if only the one called Slater and the one called Badger were still there.

Roan, Tom, and Blue had reached Helena about the same time as Paddy and Dan had ridden south out of Missoula toward Stevensville.

Rose had taken them in as if they were her own kin, and even rented a small place, an old miner's cabin, just uphill behind the Bonny Glen. She questioned them at length about what had transpired on the Lucky Seven, and filled them in as much as she could about what had happened to Dan in Helena.

When all was said and done, she cautioned Roan about going out on the street, saying that it wouldn't do to have folks find out who he was, and that he was still alive. Tom was still not right, favoring his side and having to spend a good deal of time in bed. The trip to Helena, even though only two days, had been hard on him. Rose was afraid he might have torn something open inside. But he was a good patient, and so long as he had grub when he was hungry, and Tobias, the Bonny Glen swamper, to empty the chamber pot, he was fine.

In two days Roan had read everything Rose possessed in the way of books and was pacing the floor. Blue paced with him, also ready to get out in the summer air and run.

Finally, Roan could stand it no more. He told Tom he was going up Mount Helena behind the gulch and hike about a while, and would come back without going into town.

And he did, at least half that. On the return down the mountain, he heard the fireworks. He counted on his fingers, then realized it was July third. Somebody was getting a head start on the festivities. No one could expect him to stay inside when there was fireworks.

He decided he would stay on the side streets and not go onto the main street.

Nobody in Helena knew him anyway, and he didn't know why Rose was so worried.

He and Blue would make one pass around town, get a preview of what was planned for tomorrow, then come straight back to the little cabin.

How could that hurt?

Demersville seemed a thriving, if small, town, with only two-dozen structures along the Flathead River. Its first brick building was half built, but the rest were timber and the occasional sawn plank.

A red, white, and blue banner was strung across the main street with the words GOD BLESS THE UNITED STATES. Bunting adorned the pair of coal-oil streetlights at the only intersection, and some of the fronts of the few businesses.

This time it was Dan who rode in first. He found no one but the bartender in Timber Tom's Saloon, as it was mid-morning. He moved on to a boardinghouse and café, but found the café closed and breakfast well past. At the edge of town, he found another eating establishment. A sawn-timber false front belied the much less pretentious tent rear. The cookstove was out back, under a lean-to. Two long tables were inside, with benches flanking them.

Dan, again riding Dancer, tied him out front so Paddy would know where he was, and entered. He was just finishing a mid-morning breakfast of steak and eggs when Paddy entered and limped over to the other bench. The Norwegian woman who seemed to run the place took Paddy's order, the same as Dan's had been, walked to the back and yelled it out to the cook, then came over to refill Dan's coffee, and he questioned her for the first time.

Dan gave her a big smile. "I heard a couple of friends of mine were in town. Orin Slater and Badger . . ." He mumbled the last name, as he really didn't know it.

"I don't be recognizing the names, young fella," she said, and started away.

"Wait. Slater is a tall fellow with a crooked eye, and Badger has a black beard and shaggy black hair."

"Crooked eye, eh?" She stood for a moment.

"Tall fella, crooked eye."

"I believe they was here just yesterday. They headed out of here and went to McKirdy's General Store."

"McKirdy's," Dan repeated. "I saw it on the way in. They say what they were up to?"

"Nope. I got 'nuff to do, no time to snoop into folks' business."

"Yes, ma'am." Dan spoke loud enough that Paddy could overhear. "I'll head on up to McKirdy's."

Mr. McKirdy remembered them well. "They bought four cases of whiskey, said they were headin' on up to Sprighter's."

"Sprighters?"

"There's a mill twenty-five miles upriver. Seventy or more men working there. It's a long ride into town, and they'll be wanting to hoorah the Fourth."

"I never thought of those old boys going into the saloon business."

"Actually, it was me who suggested it. I was overstocked in whiskey. They thought it a sound idea. They bought a pair of mules for the trip north, and I showed 'em a way to get the cost back."

Dan sighed. He'd thought the chase would end here. Paddy walked in about that time. "We haven't caught up with them. Another twenty-five miles."

"I got some things to buy, then we'll ride out," Paddy said.

"Hurry along. We got to ride hard to be there before nightfall. But I've got one stop to make first."

Paddy moved away, mumbling, "Good

thing I et, or I'd be getting real grouchy 'bout now."

"You're a bit on the grouchy side even with a belly full. What's eatin' at you?"

"Damned old leg hurts me a bit when I'm in the saddle for a long spell. Never did heal right."

Dan chuckled. "We are a pair to draw to. Let's get this done so we can both put our feet in front of the fire."

Dan headed for the telegraph office. He was pleased to find a wire for P.D., and opened and read it.

D.

Your package arrived safely. Can't wait for your safe arrival.

Be careful. You're in our prayers.

Rose

He was relieved, knowing Roan, Tom, and Blue were in Rose's capable hands.

It was an hour after dark when they rode into Sprighter's Mill. A side ditch fed a timber penstock with water, which fell over a hundred feet down to the mill and turned a huge water wheel, driving the mechanism in the building. The mill itself was at least eighty feet long and forty wide, mostly walled in, except for the end where they received the timber. It was winched up out of a large gathering pond where logs could be floated in from the river. Another half-dozen buildings completed the camp: a cookhouse, bunkhouses, and a small sutler's store probably owned by Sprighter, whoever he was. When they rode in, two lumberjacks were sawing away, but not on logs, on fiddles. Another twenty men were in the middle of the dirt street between the mill building and the other few, clogging to the music.

But Slater and Badger were nowhere to be seen. Dan reined up near every tall man he passed, looking for the telltale crooked eye, but none passed muster. He tied his horse in front of the sutler's, dismounted, and entered. "You're open late?" he said to the man behind the counter.

"Holiday. Fellas are wantin' lots of sodas . . . and I got firecrackers. You interested?"

"Sodas?" Dan asked. "How about whiskey?"

The man gave Dan a hard look. "This is a dry camp, friend. Against company rules. No whiskey here."

Dan shrugged, and spun on his heel, thinking that McKirdy had given Orin Slater and Badger Hotchkins good advice. Paddy had ridden in behind him and dismounted at another hitching rail, and was eying the dancers while clapping to the music and looking as if he was about to jump into the clogging contest.

Dan walked over, on the way noticing a group of men standing between two buildings and passing a bottle.

He made a sharp turn and walked over to join them.

"Can I buy a drink of that?" he asked.

A burly man as tall as Dan, but thicker, gave him a questioning look. "And who might you be?"

"Just passing through. Heard the music and thought I'd join the party. How about that drink?"

"This is a dry camp, friend. No whiskey here."

"So, that bottle's filled with lemonade."

He got another stare. "Dry camp."

"The hell you say. I want to buy a drink."

"If you're so intent on John Barlycorn, how about you buy a drink for the lot of us?" the big man said, then gave Dan a wide grin.

"That bottle won't go round another time," Dan said, eyeing the bottle being turned up by one of the lumberjacks.

"Then how about you going on up the

river a ways and finding the whiskey drummer and putting down your hard-earned for another half-dozen bottles. That should last us an hour or so, then you'll be welcome back here and again at breakfast, come morning."

"Whiskey drummer?"

"Yep, two fellas, their horses, and a pair of mules are camped up river a half mile or so. They got plenty of whiskey — if you got the price."

"Tall fellow with a crooked eye and a short stocky wild-lookin' dark-haired one?"

"That would be them," the man said, scratching his head and eying Dan. "Those highbinders would be friends of yours?"

"You might say I know of them. And I surely do want to meet them again."

"Good. Bring back some whiskey, and join the festivities."

Paddy had walked up behind Dan and overheard a good part of the conversation.

Dan turned to him. "This could be easier than I hoped for, if those two are in their cups. We can ride right up on them, and they'll be thinking we're customers from this camp."

"Then let's ride right up on them," Paddy said, flashing Dan a crooked smile. "I'm ready to end this . . . and ride for home."

It was good and dark, with the moon not up yet, when they spotted the campfire. They tied the extra horses in the brush, then continued toward the fire.

Both men were sitting near the fire, neither drinking from a bottle. Rather, Dan was disappointed to see, they were sipping coffee.

Paddy leaned closer to Dan. "Maybe I should circle around."

"And ruin all the fun? Let's do this while we're lookin' them in the eye."

"Might be hard with that old cockeyed boy," Paddy said, then laughed low.

As Dan and Paddy neared, Dan called out. "Hello the camp! You the whiskey drummers?"

"Come on in, friend, and bring your money!" the voice called back.

To Dan's chagrin, the taller of the two rose as they approached, and sauntered away from the fire, back into the shadows.

"A careful lot," Dan said to Paddy under his breath.

Paddy rode with his shotgun across the saddle. Dan left his rifle in its scabbard, but wore his Remington revolver.

Paddy remained on horseback as Dan dismounted. "Hear you've got some fine drinkin' whiskey?"

"The best," the shorter of the two said, rising from the rock where he sat.

"How much?" Dan asked.

"Two dollars the bottle."

"Two dollars!" Dan said, seeming surprised that the price was twice what it would have been in town.

"We toted it a long way, a hard load for them mules and a long ride for us," Badger said with a crooked smile.

"And those packs are well loaded down with other gear. You headed a far piece?"

"A far piece. Got charged a good bit for them mules back in Demersville. Brought the whiskey along to pay for the cost. We was headed this way anyhow. My partner's a clever man who holds a dollar close to the vest. You gonna jaw the night away, or buy some whiskey?"

"Fetch me a half-dozen bottles," Dan said.

"Show me the color of yer money," Badger replied, stepping closer.

Dan glanced up to see Paddy backing his horse away, back out of the light, trying to see where Slater was. He had the shotgun resting across his saddle horn, its muzzle aiming at the man in the shadows. Dan could barely see the man, standing just beyond the firelight, maybe fifteen paces back in the trees, but he could see him. The man stood casually, watching, his hand resting on the butt of his revolver. Dan fished a handful of coins out of his pocket, some of them gold and glistening in the firelight.

Badger nodded, then walked to where the panniers lay, dug inside, and came up with three bottles in each hand, their necks between his fingers.

It was as good a time as any. Dan drew, depending on Paddy to take the man in the shadows, leveling the Remington on Badger's chest.

Chapter 24

"You'd rob a man of a few bottles of whiskey?" Badger asked.

Then Paddy's shotgun blast roared in the quiet night. Badger dropped the bottles, and to Dan's surprise, they burst on the rocks surrounding the fire and flared in a roar, blinding Dan with the flash.

Dan fired, and spun back out of the light. His shot was returned by both the man in the trees and Badger, who'd dived behind the panniers.

Horses and mules bucked and reared and whinnied, and pounded away riderless and packless.

Suddenly, all went quiet.

Paddy was the only one left with a horse. He'd charged into the copse of tress, hunting for the one called Slater.

Dan was behind a rock, Badger twenty paces away, across the fire.

"Give it up, Badger."

"Give up my whiskey?" Badger asked. "Fat chance."

Dan smiled. "Nope, more than that. A lot more."

Badger snapped off a shot at the sound of Dan's voice. It splattered rock shards in Dan's face. He picked one out of his cheek. Dan rolled to the side, until he felt the water at the river's edge. He hoped he was far enough to the side not to be blinded by the firelight. He let his eyes adjust.

Dan heard the quick report of two shots from deeper in the copse of trees. Then the shotgun returned fire.

"Who the hell are you?" Badger called out from deep in·the darkness.

"You don't want to know," Dan said.

"Oh, yeah, I do," Badger replied. "I want to know who I'm killing. Even a dog deserves a headstone."

"You've done all the killing you're gonna do, skunk."

"The name's Badger."

"It's skunk to me."

Dan slipped on out into the river until he was chest deep, holding the revolver high, out of the water. Then he fought his way upstream until he was even with where he thought Badger was hiding. Two more shots rang out from deep in the trees; then he heard the pounding of hoofbeats, disappearing.

"Slater, you no-good pig," Badger yelled out, apparently thinking his cohort was abandoning him.

Dan took the opportunity to charge up out of the river, searching for Badger.

He was to the spot where he thought the man was hiding when a voice rang out behind him.

"I'd be throwing that iron down," Badger said. Somehow, he'd managed to slip behind Dan; maybe he too was going to the water to slip away.

Dan let the revolver turn in his hand.

"Go ahead and drop it, then tell me who I'm about to kill."

Dan turned slowly to face the man, saying nothing.

"So, who —" As Badger spoke, the brush nearby shattered aside and Paddy, still on horseback, came hard out of the tangle, his shotgun in hand.

Badger spun to face the new threat, giving Dan a half second to spin the revolver back in his grip. He fired, taking the stocky man high in the chest.

Badger turned back, firing at Dan. The bullet notched Dan's right ear, making him flinch, but he fired again, again hitting his target. Still, Badger shot at the oncoming horse and rider, and Dan fired again, this time hitting the man in the head. Badger went down hard, but with his revolver still in hand. He fired again, the shot going wild into the night sky.

Paddy was on him, and fired almost point-blank down at the man on the ground, this time blowing half of Badger's head away.

He'd fired close to the gelding's ear, and the horse began to rodeo, humping across the camp and through the campfire, kicking up a shower of sparks, which made him buck even more. He dumped Paddy like a sack of flour, but luckily, into the river's edge, then humped off into the trees.

Paddy came up out of the water, still holding his shotgun, dripping wet. "Damn if Lucifer ain't well named," Paddy managed, sputtering.

"So was this old boy," Dan said. Holding his ear with one hand, blood seeping down his cheek, he'd walked over to stare down at the man on the ground. "Tough as a damned badger. Where's the cockeyed one who's 'sposed to be the gun hand?"

"Rode off like a scalded cat, back downstream."

"Let's catch your horse and get after him, if you're finished with your bath."

"Very funny," Paddy said, but managed to give Dan a crooked smile.

"So, you'd be Roan McKeag," the thick-chested man wearing the badge asked.

Surprised to be called by name, Roan looked up to see the big man hunkering over him. "Sir?"

"Roan McKeag. You're Dan McKeag's nephew."

Roan had stayed in town much longer than he meant to, but the fireworks being tried out were just too interesting and exciting to watch, and much better as it got darker. Tomorrow night would be the big festivities. The man speaking to him was staring not at him, but at Blue.

"No, sir," Roan said. "I don't know no Dan McKeag."

"The hell you don't, boy. That's McKeag's ugly mutt, and I was told to watch out for his hands and his nephew, and that would be you. I wouldn't a known you from Adam's off ox, but I'd know that hound anywheres."

The man reached out and grabbed Roan by the arm.

Blue growled and the hair rose on his back.

The deputy marshal drew his revolver,

cocking it in the same motion, and leveled it at the big dog. "You want this dog shot down . . . like a dog?" he said, then guffawed.

"Who are you?" Roan demanded.

"Why, I'm Deputy Marshal Howard Perkins, and you — you're under arrest."

Blue moved a step or two closer to the big man.

"Blue, no," Roan said, his voice angry, but more at himself than at the dog. "You go on home."

The dog eyed Roan carefully as the deputy spoke again. "I'd shoot him, easy as pie, boy. Right between those ugly eyes. You make him settle down."

"Blue!" Roan yelled at him. "Go home!" The boy waved him away.

The big dog put his tail between his legs and moved off, but continued to watch as the big deputy dragged Roan away.

"You takin' me to jail?" Roan asked.

"No need for jail, boy. I'm gonna lock you up at my place, then I got a telegram to send."

"Why?"

" 'Cause a friend of mine will be real interested to know you're hanging about in Helena, that's why. Hell, boy, you're worth your weight in gold . . . silver at least."

"Who?"

"You're just full of questions. Bert Prager, that's who. Same fella sent me a telegram telling me to watch out for you and other no-accounts from the Lucky Seven. Now shudup."

The big deputy dragged Roan off through a dark alley.

It took Dan and Paddy over a half hour to track Paddy's horse down. Then they loaded their saddlebags with whiskey bottles and set out back to Sprighter's Mill.

The clogging was still going on when they arrived back. Men were throwing horseshoes by the light of coal-oil lamps. Others were engaged in an elimination foot race.

Dan rode directly back to the group of men in the alley, tied his horse, and removed two bottles of whiskey from the bags.

The man he'd had the conversation with turned and saw him coming. Dan smiled and handed the man the bottles.

"That earns you breakfast, lad," the man said.

"Won't be here for breakfast, friend. The tall man with the cockeye, the whiskey drummer, he come back this way?"

"He did. He rode right on through and kept moving, back Demersville way."

"Damn," Dan said.

He moved back out of the alley and saw Paddy, sitting on the edge of the board-walk, his face in his hands. He knew he'd been fading fast, about spent. "We're still on the prod."

"Damn the bloody flies. I knew I wasn't shed of this saddle yet."

"You're limping worse than ever. I want you to let me take Lucifer and the best of these two" — he nodded at the spare horse — "the dun, if I'm any judge of horseflesh, and I'm gonna ride this old boy down. If I've got two spare animals, he won't have a chance."

Paddy shook his head. "Slater's a shootist, with more notches on his revolver than that mill saw's made —"

"You're out of steam, Paddy. You can follow along behind at your own pace."

Again, Paddy shook his head. "I won't hear of it —"

"Paddy, I've been holding back. You've been holding me up."

"Bull —"

"No bull about it. I'm going on, you're resting up, then following."

"You really been holdin' back?"

"Way back. I could have run them down yesterday, with Dancer and Lucifer, without the third horse. By the time you catch up, I'll have the old boy draped over the saddle. Speaking of that, go back in the morning and strap Old Badger on one of his new mules. He's liable to be worth a couple of thousand, and you being unemployed, I'm sure you'll be needin' it. And I can use the mule on the ranch — when I get it back."

"Okay, okay. You go on, but if'n you ride out of Demersville headin' anywhere other than Missoula, you leave word with that old woman at the tent café. Understand?"

"You bet. Now give me your horse. I promise, Paddy, I'll make this end, and we'll be heading back to Deer Lodge."

"Be careful."

Dan too was exhausted, but he wouldn't let Paddy know that. Paddy had been riding the last two days, rubbing his thigh with every step. Paddy was about spent.

Dan tied the third horse to Lucifer, and led him. He nodded to his friend, Paddy, then gigged the horse into a lope.

He was sure Slater was headed back to Demersville as there was really no place else to go, at least nowhere else that was more than a game trail. What he knew of Slater, he was a townsman. He wore a frock coat and a fancy vest. He would head to town, Dan was sure of it.

It was three in the morning when Dan arrived in the little town. He was amazed that he hadn't caught Slater on the trail. He'd changed horses three times, never traveling at less than a lope. But then he realized he was very close. Slater's big gray was tied up outside the town's only livery stable, standing on three legs, his head hanging down, tongue lolling, his left foreleg swollen. It was a wonder the animal was still alive.

Dan tied his horses to the rail alongside, and walked over and gave Slater's animal a few pats on the neck. "Don't worry, boy, I'll shoot that damned Slater once for you."

He slipped into the livery, moving carefully from stall to stall, checking to see if anyone was asleep there, but there was no one. He climbed carefully into the loft, but it revealed no one either.

The livery was next door to McKirdy's, and the general store had a bench and a pair of chairs on the boardwalk. Dan walked there, seated himself, and waited.

He was tired. He put his feet up on one chair, and decided to rest his eyes.

He awoke with a start, the sun full up.

There was a man standing in the dirt street. Dan could barely see him, as the man had the morning sun at his back.

"Get up, you sum'bitch. You been running me like a damn dog, and it's gonna stop here."

"Slater?" Dan asked, shading his eyes with a hand.

"Orin Slater, and how do you know that and who the hell are you? You got no badge."

There was a small crowd beginning to form. Dan wondered why Slater hadn't shot him down where he sat, then figured he had too many witnesses. Besides, Slater thought he was the toughest, and fastest, bull in the corral.

Dan slowly rose, then moved slightly to the side so the sun was out of his eyes.

"I'm Dan McKeag, Slater. You remember that name, don't you?"

Chapter 25

"I do" — he spit on the ground between them — "and that makes this a lot more interesting. I thought you was some law dog, but you're just another cowhand, one that's worth a pocketful of money to me." As Slater spoke, he pulled his frock coat back over the butt of a nickel-plated Smith and Wesson Russian Model revolver on his hip.

"You know, we've got something in common," Dan said as he moved into the street.

"What's that?"

"You're worth a pocketful of money to me."

"How so?"

"Reward. You're right, I'm no law dog, but you're wanted dead or alive, and I can collect, law dog or no."

"Then pull that iron so I can shoot you down legal-like."

Dan smiled. "You're too damn fast for me, Slater. I've heard about you. I think I'll just turn around and walk away this time. I'll catch up to you some other time, maybe when you're drunk, or sleeping."

The crowd was growing, and a low murmur moved through them as they tried to figure out what was going on in their street.

"We don't allow no guns in town," one of them called out. Slater kept his eyes on Dan.

"You hear that, Slater? You're breaking the law again."

"To hell with the law," Slater said. He was clenching and unclenching his right hand, about to reach.

"And there John Law comes," Dan said, motioning with his head.

It was enough to get Slater's attention away for a instant.

As Slater cut his eyes, Dan grabbed for his revolver. Slater was fast. His attention back on Dan, he drew so quickly his revolver cleared leather and discharged first. But Dan dropped to one knee, and the shot blew his hat off. Dan's Remington spit flame and took Slater dead center in the chest. He windmilled back and fell flat, puffing up a cloud of dust.

Dan rose and approached him. Slater still held the revolver, and tried to lift it. Dan fired again, point-blank into Slater's chest.

"The first one was for Erin and the others; that one was for that poor horse you rode down."

But Slater wasn't answering. This time his hand had gone slack, and the revolver slipped away into the dust.

"Drop that firearm," a commanding voice said.

Dan let it hang at his side, turning to see a tall man wearing a badge on his starched white shirt. Dan let the revolver fall into the dirt.

Dan nodded at the man. "I've got a letter for you, marshal. From Houston Greenlaw, over in Deer Lodge."

"Marshal Greenlaw?"

"One and the same."

It took Dan an hour to settle things with the Demersville marshal and get a statement from him regarding Slater's death. It was almost noon when he went to the tent restaurant, ate a fine venison stew while he waited for Paddy, then when Paddy didn't show, left word with the woman that he was on his way back to Deer Lodge.

Tom and Rose searched Helena by horseback, then the town afoot when Blue returned without Roan. Tom was spent and had to return to rest, hoping Roan would show up back at the cabin.

The boy was nowhere to be found. Finally, Rose went to see Marshal Harbin Smyth. Neither the marshal nor any of his deputies knew anything about the boy. Finally, Rose went to the telegraph office and wired Marshal Houston Greenlaw, thinking that the boy might have decided to return to the Lucky Seven and knew neither of them would have given permission.

With no other leads, they decided all they could do was wait.

Roan had been kept in the dark, hands tied, locked in a closet. He hadn't heard any sounds for hours as he struggled to free himself; then he heard footfalls outside.

The door opened and light flooded him. He squinted, then realized it was the same ugly deputy who'd brought him here.

"I'm hungry," Roan said.

"We'll eat on the trail."

"The trail?"

"Yep, we're heading for Deer Lodge."

"How come?"

"Mr. Prager wants me to deliver you there, just like you was a side of beef."

Dan led two fine horses and had a strong well-rested one under him when he sat out south to Big Fork, stopping only for minutes at the half-breed settlement and Polkinghorn's Trading Post where the river entered Flathead Lake, then followed Mullen's trail of 1854 and the Swan River southeast. He made sixty miles before he camped in the high lonely. Crossing a saddle in between the Mission Mountains and the higher and even wilder mountains to the east, he picked up the headwaters of the Clearwater. He kept moving south until he found the Blackfoot, then rode upriver until he saw what looked like a pass to the south. He camped again on a divide looking down on the Hell's Gate River, and knew he was close to Deer Lodge.

It was noon when he loped up on a ridge overlooking the Bar X buildings. A half-dozen hands worked about the barn and corrals.

Dan dismounted and studied the situation below. He'd been riding hard for two and a half days. He was alone. Bert Prager was below, but he had as many as twenty hands surrounding him.

He wanted this confrontation more than almost anything, but not more than living to finish it. He had to use his head. He remounted and moved back up into a thick copse of lodgepole pine. It was warm, and he and the horses welcomed the shade. He decided to rest, and wait for dark.

It was late in the afternoon when Howard Perkins rode into the Bar X and tied up at the hitching rail outside the main house. He untied the youth's legs from the stirupps and jerked the boy from the saddle, letting him sprawl in the dirt. Then he gave him a kick, fed up with the trouble he'd been given during the two-day ride from Helena.

One of the Bar X hands was nearby, and had been looking on curiously when they'd ridden up. Seeing the boy being mistreated, he hurried over. "Here now, what's going on?"

Perkins turned so the man could see the deputy marshal's badge pinned to his waistcoat. "This is law business, friend. I'd suggest you butt out."

The ranch hand studied the situation for a moment. "I don't know nothin' about no law business, but even if the law's gonna hang this youngster, you got no reason to beat him around."

Perkins eyed the man. "Unless you want to go to town in irons, you'll butt out."

The man finally spun on his heel and headed toward the barn, disgusted, but not so much he'd risk a run-in with the law.

Perkins grabbed the boy by the collar, jerked him to his feet, and dragged him up to and in the house.

Elga directed them into the parlor. She too was taken aback by the treatment the young man was receiving. She knew the boy, at least well enough to know who he was.

But Prager snapped at her, telling her to go about her business.

The old man smiled at Perkins. "You did right good, Howard." He fished his strongbox out from under the desk, opened it, and handed the promised hundred dollars to the deputy marshal.

Perkins gave him a grin.

"You ain't quite done," Prager said. "Take him down to the tater cellar and tie him up good. I'll deal with him later."

Perkins did as told, then left and headed back to Helena.

Prager had a problem. The boy was alive. Badger had lied to him. He had to have a little chat with the boy, find out what he knew and who else might be left from the Lucky Seven crew. He was fresh out of hands who would deal with something like what had to be done with the boy, if he'd seen enough to testify against any of the Bar X hands, or even ex-hands. Prager suspected the boy had seen far too much, and Prager knew he couldn't leave the boy alive.

As Perkins rode out, Elga appeared in Prager's office doorway. "Would you like a cup of tea, Mr. Prager?"

Prager looked up from his books. "No, Elga, leave me be."

She was quiet for a long moment. "You got that young boy down in the cellar —"

"That's none of your business, Elga. Go on now."

Again, she was silent for a long moment. "I have to live here too, Bert. I don't want that boy hurt."

Prager jerked up, then rose so quickly he about lost his balance and fell. "Damn you, woman. I'm Mr. Prager to you. You get back —"

She interrupted him, something she'd never done before. Her eyes flared in anger as she spoke. "By God, Bert Prager, I do for you, just like a wife. And I don't want no youngster hurt, or worse, where I abide."

"Then by all that's holy, you'll abide some-by-God-place else. You pack your things and get the hell out."

She looked as if she'd been slapped. "You'd throw me out?"

"You are throwed out. You pack up, and I'll have you driven into town in the morning. Ain't no little poke once in a while gonna make you the empress of the manor."

She reddened so much that Prager thought she might have apoplexy, but she spun on her heel and stomped away.

Prager yelled after her. "And by God, you'll fix my supper tonight and my breakfast in the morning, or I'll throw you out right now and you'll walk to town, dragging your carpetbag behind you, understand?"

"I'll fix your supper, you old bastard," she said, but her words trailed off as she disappeared into the kitchen.

Prager was so angry he couldn't return to his books, so he hobbled to the window and watched the men work about the place. Finally, he hobbled back to his chair. After the woman left for town, he'd take care of the boy, and bury him right there in the damn cellar. Then he'd go about finding another hand who could come to work for him and do that kind of dirty work, and another housekeeper.

Damn woman was way too uppity for her own good.

He went back to his books.

Dan was well rested when the sun settled behind the Flint Range to the west. He rigged a picket line with his reata and tied Lucifer and the other mount where they could graze, saddled Dancer, then headed down the long slope to the Bar X buildings and corrals, threading his way between a small herd of cows and calves.

He approached the house on the far side from the hands' bunkhouse and cookshack. Taking a deep breath, he studied the house. The housekeeper worked in the kitchen, preparing the old man's supper, Dan presumed. But there seemed to be no one else about. Dan slipped up on the back porch, watching her as she dished up a bowl of soup, then disappeared through a door. Unless she ate alone in the main dining room, which Dan doubted, the old man was there.

Dan moved far enough to the edge of the porch that he could see into a dining-room window. Sure enough, Old Man Prager hobbled into the room, took a seat, and picked up a soup spoon.

Dan was both sorry and happy that the woman was there. He planned to confront Prager with what he knew, and make the man confess, and he needed a witness. But most of all, he needed to kill the son of a bitch. No matter what else, Prager needed to pay.

Bert Prager had begun to think about Elga — not about forgiving her, that was the last thing on his mind — but rather about how angry she was and what she knew about things that went on around the Bar X. He'd finally come to the conclusion that she could be run off without much risk. After all, who'd believe a fat old housekeeper against the word of Bertoldus Prager? No one, that's who.

But what else was she capable of? He wouldn't put it past her to try and shove a kitchen knife between his ribs. He'd never seen anyone quite so angry as she'd appeared when he told her to pack up, and he'd seen a lot of angry folks in his time.

Just as a precaution, he jammed his little Smith and Wesson .41-caliber Thunderer into his belt, loosening his shirt so it would be out of sight.

Dan waited until the woman moved out of the kitchen again, responding to Prager's demanding yell. Then he slipped in the back door.

He could hear voices from the dining room.

"You take a spoonful of that slop, woman."

"You think I done poisoned you, Bert?"

"Don't call me Bert. Just take a spoonful."

Dan smiled, listening to the exchange. The old man was getting senile, having to have a court taster for his food now. The evil old son of a bitch probably needed one.

"There," she said.

Dan stepped aside as she pushed her way back into the kitchen.

She gasped when she saw him, and he expected her to scream, but she didn't. She looked him up and down, then went to her stove, opened the oven, and took out a roast.

Dan pushed into the dining room. He didn't bother to palm the Remington, as he'd seen Prager enter the room, and he was unarmed.

"Ain't bad soup," Prager said without looking up.

"Enjoy it," Dan said. "It's your last meal."

Prager snapped his eyes up. To Dan's surprise, his eyes flared for a moment in surprise, then he smiled. "Why, if it ain't my good neighbor, Dan McKeag, back from the dead."

Dan eyed the old man, who was beginning to look, and act, a little crazy in his old age. His salt-and-pepper hair and beard were wild and unkempt. His beard was stained with tobacco juice. He looked like the last one who should be seated in this dining room in this fine house.

"Bertoldus, I am back from the dead, and it's my full intention to send you over to the other side. You're an evil old bastard and you're gonna rot in hell for all time for what you've done to me and mine."

The old man cackled. "You wanna join me for dinner, Danny me lad?"

"I wouldn't sit at the same table with evil scum such as you, nor would I eat your food."

The door behind Dan pushed open, and the housekeeper appeared. "I'd like to make you a plate, Mr. McKeag."

Dan shook his head, then glanced back at Bert Prager. The old man was smiling as evilly as the devil himself and holding a small revolver, leveled at Dan's middle.

"You never was smart as a gopher, McKeag. Now who's crossing over to the other side?"

Dan smirked at the old man. "You know, Bertoldus, that little revolver of yours doesn't hold enough bullets to keep me from pulling this Remington and blowing you into hell."

As he spoke, the fat housekeeper pushed her way past Dan. She held a platter in one hand; her other was tucked under her apron. She moved around the table, the platter full of sliced roast beef.

"Elga, get the hell out of here," Prager demanded.

"Why, Bert, I got your favorite," she said.

Dan had to make his move if he wanted to walk, or even crawl, away from this. Maybe the woman moving around the table was the distraction he needed. But Prager never took his eyes off Dan.

She moved up beside Bert, sat the platter down, removed the soup bowl from his dinner plate, took a two-pronged serving fork in hand, and forked two generous slabs of roast beef onto his plate.

"Damn it, Elga —" he started to berate her; then his complaint was cut short as she jammed the fork through his beard and deep into his throat.

Dan was almost too surprised to draw his gun; then Prager's little Thunderer blasted. But the shot was wild, into the ceiling. With his slow left hand, Dan pulled his weapon, but the big woman had shoved Prager out of his chair, sprawling him on the floor.

"Bastard, bastard," she yelled, bending over him.

Dan rounded the table as Prager's revolver fired again, and the woman stumbled back.

The Remington roared, but too late to save the woman, who was shot in her large bosum. Dan fired again, at point-blank range, as Prager tried to cock the Thunderer again.

Then Dan kicked the weapon away. He stepped over Prager and went to the woman, who lay on the floor, holding her chest.

"Don't talk," Dan said. "I'll get something —"

But she interrupted him. "The boy, the boy is locked in the cellar. That . . . that deputy . . . Perkins . . . he . . . brought . . . him here. The old bastard had . . . had . . . evil on his mind."

"Don't talk," Dan said, then turned back to see Prager, blood running from his mouth onto his beard, but he was again reaching for his gun. Dan again kicked it away.

"You know, Bertoldus, I'd shoot you again and put you out of your misery, but that would be too easy. Die hard, you filthy old man."

But the old man died still smiling. And a few breaths later, the woman followed.

Dan had started moving out of the room when the front door burst open and a pair of ranch hands filled the doorway. Dan leveled the Remington on them.

"Prager's dead. He shot the housekeeper, who stabbed him with her fork, and I shot him. I'd say the Bar X is out of business. You all can stay here for as long as you want, until the law comes along and runs you off. I'm Dan McKeag, and I own the ranch next door, no matter what this old thief might have told you. I'll be hiring, and six or seven of the best of you can get on there, after I return from Helena . . . or you can die where you stand."

The men in the doorway stood silent for a moment; then one of them spoke up. "I know you, McKeag, and have never heard a bad word about you — 'cept'n from Old Man Prager here — and I never put much stock in his opinion of folks. I'm going on out and telling the boys that the old man finally got what was coming to him. I doubt you'll have trouble from any of them. I'll be over to see you in a few days . . . after I take a little time off in Deer

Lodge and get the taste of this rotten old bastard out of my mouth with some cheap whiskey."

Dan nodded, not surprised that a Prager Bar X hand had no problem riding away from the brand — in fact, even seemed anxious to do so. Then Dan hurried out through the kitchen to where he'd seen the cellar door, which opened off the back of the house. True to the housekeeper's last words, he found Roan tied up there.

Epilogue

Dan, Roan, and Paddy attended the trial of Al Givens in Missoula and, thanks to the convincing testimony of Roan, watched him hang two days later. Dan took little pleasure in the spectacle, but it seemed a fitting end to the summer's troubles.

Paddy used a good portion of the reward money, two thousand each for Slater and Givens, and to his surprise, five thousand for Badger Hotchkins — who was wanted for murder in far-off California — to purchase the Bonny Glen from Rose Ballard, who no longer needed the place. She had a fine new house to live in, and a man who took all of her time to cook and care for.

It turned out that Bert Prager had a substantial loan at the Helena Stockmen and Merchants Bank, and Dan's old friend, Silas Bingham, was more than happy to have neighbor Dan McKeag assume that loan and take over the ownership of the Bar X, which Dan merged into the Lucky Seven. There was no more Bertoldus

Prager, nor a Bar X ranch. Most of the Bar X hands stayed on with Dan, not even having to move their gear from the bunkhouse.

As his last official act before he retired — a retirement suggested by the territorial governor when he learned the facts — Judge Oscar Pettibone Harley set aside the forged deed and reinstated Dan McKeag as sole owner of the Lucky Seven.

Dan was pleased to give Kelly Dugan a job as ramrod of the Lucky Seven, as there was more than enough work for all of them, and Meegan Dugan was employed part-time to help with the big house and cook. Tom was stove up and not up to the hours in the saddle the job of ramrod required. Tom became the saddle and tack man for the ranch, a job only requiring the morning hours.

A year and a week after Erin's death, Roan stood as best man at the wedding of Rose Ballard and Dan McKeag.

And the McKeag family now owned all of McKeag's Mountain.